"Riot on the Street of Gods!"

The voice of the Guard's communications sorcerer boomed suddenly in Hawk and Fisher's minds: *Riot on the Street of Gods! All available personnel report to the Street of Gods immediately. This command overrides all other orders and priorities until further notice.*

Hawk and Fisher scrambled to their feet, their hands clawing instinctively for their weapons. The God Squad were on their feet too, looking equally shocked. They'd picked up the message, too. The informer rose uncertainly to his feet.

"My friends, what is it? What has happened?"

"It seems your information came a little too late this time," said Rowan. "Someone's just fired the first shot in a God War."

She ran out the door, with Tomb close behind her.

Hawk turned to Buchan. "You're the expert. What's the best thing to do?"

"Pray," said Buchan. "But make sure you pick the right God."

Ace Books by Simon R. Green

HAWK AND FISHER
WINNER TAKES ALL
THE GOD KILLER

WOLF IN THE FOLD
(Coming in September)

HAWK & FISHER

THE GOD KILLER

SIMON R. GREEN

ACE BOOKS, NEW YORK

This book is an Ace original edition,
and has never been previously published.

THE GOD KILLER

An Ace Book / published by arrangement with
the author

PRINTING HISTORY
Ace edition / June 1991

ISBN: 0-441-29460-X

Ace Books are published by The Berkley Publishing Group,
200 Madison Avenue, New York, New York 10016.
The name "ACE" and the "A" logo
are trademarks belonging to Charter Communications, Inc.

PRINTED IN THE UNITED STATES OF AMERICA

10 9 8 7 6 5 4 3 2 1

Prologue

They come and they go.

There are Beings on the Street of Gods. More and less than human, they inspire worship and adoration, fear and awe, and dreams of endless power. No one knows who or what the Beings are. They existed before men built the Street of Gods, and will exist long after the Street is nothing more than rubble and memories. Some say the Beings are distillations of specific realities; abstract concepts given shape and form by human fears or wishes, or simply by the times themselves. Others claim they are simply supernatural creatures, intrusions from other planes of existence. No one knows. They are real and unreal, both and neither. They are Beings of Power, and the Street of Gods is theirs and theirs alone.

They come and they go.

1

Killer on the Loose

Winter had come early to the city port of Haven, ushered in on blustering winds full of sleet and snow and bitter cold. Thick blankets of snow lay heavily across the roofs and city walls, and hoarfrost pearled the brickwork. Down in the street, the first of the day's pedestrian traffic struggled through the muddy slush, slipping and sliding and cursing each other through numb lips. The cold wind cut through the thickest furs, and frostbite gnawed savagely at exposed flesh. Winter had come to Haven, and honed its cutting edge on the slow-moving and the infirm.

It was early in the morning, the sun little more than a bloody promise on the starless night. The street lamps glowed bravely against the dark, islands of amber light in an endless gloom. Ruddy lanterns hung from horses and carts, bobbing like live coals on the night. And trudging through the cold and dark came Hawk and Fisher, husband and wife and Captains in the city Guard. Somewhere up ahead in the narrow streets and alleyways of the Northside lay a dead man. It wasn't clear yet why he was dead. Apparently the investigating Constables were still trying to find some of the pieces.

Murder was nothing new in the Northside. Every city has a dark and cruel side to its nature, and Haven was no different. Haven was a dark city, the rotten apple of the Low

Kingdoms, but murder and corruption flourished openly in the Northside, fuelled by greed and hate and bitter need. People died there every day for reasons of passion, desperation, or business. Nevertheless, this latest in a line of bloody murders had shocked even the hardened Northsiders. So the Guard sent in Hawk and Fisher. There wasn't much that could shock them.

Hawk was tall, dark, but no longer handsome. A series of old scars ran down the right side of his face, and a black silk patch covered his right eye. He wore a long furred jacket and trousers and a heavy black Guardsman's cloak. He didn't look like much. He was lean and wiry rather than muscular, and he was beginning to build a stomach. He wore his long dark hair swept back from his forehead and tied with a silver clasp at the nape. He had only just turned thirty, but already there were streaks of grey in his hair. It would have been easy to dismiss Hawk as just another bravo, perhaps a little past his prime and going to seed, but there was something about Hawk; something hard and unyielding and almost sinister. People walked quietly around him, and were careful to keep their voices calm and reasonable. On his right hip Hawk carried a short-handled axe instead of a sword. He was very good with an axe. He'd had lots of practice in his five years as a Guard.

Isobel Fisher walked at Hawk's side, echoing his pace and stance with the naturalness of long companionship. She was tall, easily six feet in height, lithely muscular, and her long blond hair fell to her waist in a single thick plait, weighted at the tip with a polished steel ball. She was in her mid- to late-twenties, and handsome rather than beautiful. There was a rawboned harshness to her face which contrasted strongly with her deep blue eyes and generous mouth. Somewhere in the past, something had scoured all the human weaknesses out of her, and it showed. Like Hawk, she wore the Guard's standard uniform for winter, with a sword at her left hip. Her hand rested comfortably on the pommel.

A thin mist hung about the street, though the weather wizards had been trying to clear it for hours. The cold seeped relentlessly into Hawk's bones as he strode along, and he stamped his boots hard into the slush to try and keep some warmth in his feet. His hands were curled into fists inside his gloves, but it didn't seem to be helping much. Hawk hated the cold, hated the way it leached all the warmth and life out of him. And in particular, he hated being out in the cold and the dark at such an ungodly hour of the morning. But this shift paid the best, and he and Fisher needed the money, so . . . Hawk shrugged irritably, trying to get his cloak to fall more comfortably about him. He hated wearing a cloak; it always got in the way during fights. But braving the winter cold without a cloak was about as sensible as skinny-dipping in an alligator pool; you tended to lose important parts of your anatomy. So Hawk wore his cloak, and moaned about it a lot. He shrugged his shoulders again, and tugged surreptitiously at the cloak's hem.

"Leave that cloak alone," said Fisher, without looking at him. "It looks fine."

Hawk sniffed. "It doesn't feel right. The day's supposed to get warmer, anyway. If the mists clear up, I think I might drop the cloak off somewhere and pick it up at the end of the shift."

"You'll do no such thing. You know you get colds and flus easily, and I'm not nursing you through another one of those. A couple of degrees of fever and you think you're dying."

Hawk stared straight ahead, pretending he hadn't heard that. "Where is this body we're supposed to look at, anyway?"

"Silver Street. Just down here, on the left. It sounded fairly gruesome. Do you suppose it'll look like the others?"

"I hope so," said Hawk. "I'd hate to think there was more than one homicidal maniac running around on our patch."

Fisher nodded glumly. "I hate maniacs. They don't play by the rules. Trying to figure out their motives is enough to drive you crazy."

Hawk smiled slightly, but the smile didn't last long. If this corpse was as bad as the others he'd seen, it wasn't going to be a pretty sight. A Guard Constable had found the first body down by the Devil's Hook, hanging from a lamppost on a rope made from its own intestines. The second body had been found scattered the length of Hawthorne Alley. The killer had got inventive with the third victim, on Lower Eel Street. The hands had been nailed to a wall. The head was found floating in a water butt. There was no trace of the body's genitals.

Hawk and Fisher turned into Silver Street, and found a crowd already gathered despite the early hour. Nothing like a good murder to bring out a crowd. Hawk wondered briefly what the hell all these people were doing out on the streets at such an unearthly hour, but he knew better than to ask. They'd only lie. The Northside never slept. There was always somebody ready to make a deal, and someone else ready to cheat him.

Hawk and Fisher pushed their way through the crowd. Some of the sightseers reacted angrily at being jostled out of the way, but quickly fell silent as they recognised the two Guards. Everyone in the Northside knew Hawk and Fisher. Hawk paused briefly at the thick line of blue chalk dust the Guard Doctor had laid down to keep the crowd back, and then he took a deep breath and walked quickly over it. The silver torc at his wrist, his badge of office, protected him from the ward's magic, but the blue line always made him nervous. He'd once made the mistake of crossing the line on a day he'd absent-mindedly left his torc at home, and the agonising muscle cramps had lasted the best part of an hour. Which was why the crowd had pushed right up to the edge of the line but made no move to cross it. Thus ensuring that the scene of the crime remained intact and the Guard Doctor had room to work.

A Guard Constable was standing by, at a respectful distance from the body. His dark red cloak and tunic looked almost garish against the winter snow. He nodded affably to Hawk and Fisher. The Doctor was squatting in the blood-stained snow beside the body, but rose to his feet to nod briefly to the two Captains. He was a short, delicate man with pale face and eyes and large, clever hands. His official cloak was too large for him and looked like a hand-me-down, but he had the standard look of calm assurance that all doctors seem to be issued along with their diplomas.

"I'm glad you're here, Captain Hawk, Captain Fisher. I'm Dr. Jaeger. I haven't had much time with the body yet, but I can tell you this much: The killer didn't use a weapon. He did all this with his bare hands."

Hawk looked at the body, and had to fight to keep his face impassive. The arms had been torn out of their sockets. The torso had been ripped open from throat to groin and the internal organs pulled out and strewn across the bloody snow. The legs had been broken repeatedly. Jagged splinters of bone pierced the tattered skin. There was no sign of the head.

"Hell's teeth." Hawk tried to imagine how much sheer strength was needed to destroy a body so completely, and a disturbing thought came to him. "Doctor, is there any chance this could have been a nonhuman assailant? Werewolf, vampire, ghoul?"

Jaeger shook his head firmly. "There's no evidence of blood drainage; you can see for yourself how much there is around the body. There's no tooth or claw marks to indicate a shapeshifter. And apart from the missing head, everything's here somewhere. No evidence of feasting. No, Captain, the odds are this is your standard homicidal maniac, with a very nasty disposition."

"Great," said Fisher. "Just great. How long before the forensic sorcerer gets here?"

Jaeger shrugged. "Your guess is as good as mine. He's been contacted, but you know how he hates to be dragged from his nice warm bed at this hour of the morning."

"All right," said Hawk. "We can't wait; the trail will get cold. We'd better use your magic to get things started, Doctor. How much can you do?"

"Not a lot," Jaeger admitted. "When he finally gets here, the forensic sorcerer might be able to re-create the entire killing and show us exactly what happened. The best I can give you is a glimpse of the killer's face."

"That's more than we've got from the last three killings," said Hawk.

"We were lucky with this one," said Jaeger. "Death couldn't have taken place more than half an hour ago. The chances of scrying the face are very good."

"Wait a minute," said Fisher. "I thought you needed the head for that, so you could see the killer's face in the victim's eyes?"

Jaeger smiled condescendingly. "Medical sorcery has progressed far beyond those old superstitions, Captain Fisher." He knelt down beside the body again, grimacing as the bloody slush stained his clothes, and bent over the torso. The fingers of his left hand moved slowly in a complex pattern, and he muttered something short and guttural under his breath. Blood gushed suddenly from the neck of the torso, spilling out in a steady stream to form a wide pool. Jaeger gestured abruptly, and the blood stopped flowing. Ripples spread slowly across the pool, as though disturbed by something under the surface. Hawk and Fisher watched, fascinated, as a face slowly formed in the blood. The features were harsh, brooding, and quite distinct. Hawk and Fisher bent forward and studied the face thoroughly, committing it to memory. The image suddenly disappeared, and the blood was only blood again. Hawk and Fisher straightened up, and Jaeger got to his feet again. Hawk nodded appreciatively to him.

"Anything else you can do for us?"

"Not really. From the pattern of the bloodstains, I don't think the victim had time to struggle much. Which suggests that most if not all the mutilations took place after death."

"Cause of death?" said Fisher.

Jaeger shrugged. "Take your pick. Any one of those injuries would have been enough to kill him."

Hawk gestured for the Guard Constable to come over and join them. He was a dark, heavy-set man in his mid-forties, with a twenty-year star on his uniform. He had the calm, resigned look of the seasoned Guard who'd seen it all before and hadn't been impressed then, either. He glanced briefly at the body as he came to stand beside it, but nothing showed in his face.

"Constable Roberts at your service, Captain Hawk, Captain Fisher."

"Who found the body?" said Hawk.

"Couple of kids coming back from a party. Merchant families. Took a shortcut through the Northside on a dare, and found a bit more than they bargained for. They're in the house opposite with my partner, having a cup of tea. It's good for shock, tea."

"They see anything, apart from the body?"

"Apparently not, Captain."

"We'd better have a word with them, anyway. See if you can move that crowd along. The forensic sorcerer should be here soon, and he hates working in front of an audience."

The Constable nodded, and Hawk and Fisher headed for the house he'd indicated, stepping around the bloodstains where they could.

"You know," said Fisher quietly, "it's times like this I seriously think about getting out of this job. You think you've seen every nasty sight and spectacle the Northside can throw at you, and then something like this happens. How can one human being do that to another?"

Hawk felt like shrugging, but didn't. It had been a serious question. "Drugs. Passion. Possession. Maybe just plain crazy. There are all sorts in the Northside, on their way up or on their way down. If a man's got any darkness in his soul, the Northside will bring it out. Don't take it so personally, Isobel. We've seen worse. Just concentrate on finding the clues that will help us nail the bastard."

The young couple who'd found the body were still in the house where they'd been left, too shocked and disorientated even to think about making a fuss about leaving. They were clearly merchant-class by their dress, lower-middle by the look of them, and looked distinctly out of place in the dim smoky kitchen, being fussed over by a motherly washerwoman. Another Guard Constable was sitting comfortably by the fire, keeping an eye on them. He wore a ten-year star, but looked like he'd spent most of those years indoors. He nodded pleasantly to Hawk and Fisher, but made no move to get up. The merchant boy looked to be in his late teens, the girl a year or two younger. Hawk drew up a chair opposite them, and concentrated his questions on the boy. The girl was half asleep in her chair, worn out by shock and emotional exhaustion.

"I'm Captain Hawk, of the city Guard. This is my partner, Captain Fisher. What's your name, lad?"

"Fairfax, sir. Calvin Fairfax."

"All right, Calvin, tell us about finding the body."

Fairfax swallowed once, and nodded stiffly. "We were walking down Wool Street, Belinda and I, when we heard something. Footsteps, like someone running away. Then Belinda saw spots of blood on the ground, leading into the next street. She didn't want to get involved, but I thought we should at least take a look, in case someone was injured and needed help. We walked a little way down the street . . . and that's when we saw the body."

"Did you see anyone else in Silver Street?" said Fisher.

"No. There was no one else there. Belinda screamed, but no one came to help. A few people looked out their windows at us, but they didn't want to get involved. Finally the Guard Constables heard her, and came to see what was happening."

Fisher nodded understandingly. "What time was this?"

"About three o'clock. I heard the tower bell sound the hour not long before. The Constables took over once they saw the body. We've been waiting here ever since. Can we go now, please? We're very late. Our parents will be worried."

"In a while," said Hawk. "The forensic sorcerer will want to see you, when he finally gets here, but after that you're free to go. You'll have to make a statement for the Coroner's Court, but you can do that any time. And in future, stay out of the Northside. This isn't a safe place to be walking about, especially early in the morning."

"Don't worry," said Fairfax earnestly, "I never want to see this place again for the rest of my life. We wouldn't have come this way anyway if Luther hadn't dared us to walk past the Bode house."

Hawk's ears pricked up. The Bode house. The name rang a faint but very definite bell. "What's so special about the Bode house?"

Fairfax shrugged. "It's supposed to be haunted. People have seen things, heard things. We thought it would be a lark." His mouth twisted sourly. "We thought it would be fun. . . ."

Hawk talked reassuringly with him for a while, and then he and Fisher left the house and walked back down Silver Street. The cold morning air seemed even harsher after the comfortable warmth of the kitchen.

"Bode house . . . " Hawk frowned thoughtfully. "I know that name from somewhere."

"You should do," said Fisher. "It's been mentioned in our briefings for the past three nights. There are some indications the place may be haunted. Neighbours have complained of strange lights and sounds, and no one's seen the occupant for days. Since Bode is an alchemist and a sorcerer, no one's taking it too seriously yet, but there's no doubt it's got the neighbours rattled."

"Beats me how you can take in all that stuff," said Hawk. "It's all I can do to keep my eyes open at the beginning of the shift. I don't really wake up till I've been on the streets an hour."

"Don't think I haven't noticed," said Fisher.

"Where is this Bode house?"

"Just down the street and round the corner."

Hawk stopped and looked at her. "Coincidence?"

"Could be."

"I don't believe in coincidence. I think we'd better take a look, just to be sure."

"Might be a good idea to have a word with Constable Roberts first," said Fisher. "This is his particular territory; he might know something useful."

Hawk looked at her approvingly. "You're on the ball today, lass."

Fisher grinned. "One of us has to be."

As it turned out, Constable Roberts wasn't much help.

"Can't tell you anything definite about the house, Captains. I've heard a few things, but there are always rumors with a sorcerer's house. Bode's a quiet enough fellow; lives alone and keeps himself to himself. No one's seen him for a while, but that's not unusual. He often goes off on journeys. Since no one's been actually hurt or threatened, I've just let the place be. Bode wouldn't thank me for sticking my nose into his business, and I'm not getting a sorcerer mad at me for no good reason."

Hawk's mouth tightened, and for a moment he almost said something, but in the end he let it go. Looking out for Number One was standard practice in Haven, even amongst the Guard. Especially amongst the Guard. "Fair enough, Constable. I think we'll take a look anyway. You stay here until the forensic sorcerer arrives. And keep your eyes open. The killer could still be around here somewhere."

He got exact directions from Roberts, and then he and Fisher pushed their way through the thinning crowd and set off down the street. It wasn't far. The sorcerer's house was set on the end of a row of fairly well-preserved tenements. Not too impressive, but not bad for the area. The window shutters were all firmly closed, and there was no sign of any light. Hawk tried to feel any uneasy atmosphere that might be hanging about the place, but either there wasn't one or he was so cold by now he couldn't feel it. He took off his right glove and slipped his hand inside his shirt. Hanging around his neck on a silver chain was a carved bone amulet. Standard issue for all Guards, the amulet could detect the presence of magic anywhere nearby. He held the amulet firmly in his hand, but the small piece of bone was still and quiet. As far as it was concerned, there was no magic at all in the vicinity. Which was unusual, to say the least. A sorcerer's house should be crawling with defensive spells. He took his hand away and quickly pulled his glove back on, flexing his numbed fingers to drive out the cold.

"Have you got the suppressor stone?" he asked quietly.

"I thought you'd get round to that," said Fisher. "You've been dying to try the thing out, haven't you?"

Hawk shrugged innocently. The suppressor stone was the latest bright idea from the Council's circle of sorcerers. They weren't standard issue yet, but a number of Guards had volunteered to try them out. Working the streets of Haven, a Guard needed every helpful device he could get his hands on. Theoretically, the suppressor stone was capable of cancelling out all magic within its area of influence. In practice, the range was very limited; it misfired as often as it worked, and they still weren't sure about side effects. Hawk couldn't wait to try it out. He loved new gadgets.

Which was why Fisher carried the stone.

"Great big overgrown kid," she muttered under her breath.

Hawk smiled, walked up to the front door and studied it warily. It looked ordinary enough. There was a fancy brass door-knocker, but Hawk didn't try it. Probably booby-trapped. Sorcerers were a suspicious lot. He knelt down suddenly as something caught his eye. Someone had used the iron boot-scraper recently. There was mud and slush and a few traces of blood. Hawk smiled, and straightened up. Sooner or later, they always made a mistake. You just had to be sharp enough to spot it. He looked at Fisher, and she nodded to show she'd seen it too. They both drew their weapons. Hawk hammered on the door twice with the butt of his axe. The loud, flat sound echoed on the quiet. There was no response.

"All right," said Hawk. "When in doubt, be direct." He lifted his axe to strike at the door, but Fisher stopped him.

"Hold it, Hawk. We could be wrong. If by some chance the sorcerer has come home, and is just a slow answerer, he's not going to look too kindly on us if we break his door down. And if that isn't him in there, why warn him we're coming? I've got a better way."

She reached into a hidden pocket and pulled out a set of lock-picks. She bent over the door lock, fiddled expertly for a few seconds, and then pushed the door quietly ajar. Hawk looked impressed.

"You've been practicing."

Fisher grinned. "Never know when it might come in handy."

Hawk pushed the door open, revealing a dark, empty hall. He and Fisher stood where they were, weapons at the ready, studying the hallway.

"There's bound to be some kind of security spell, to keep strangers out," said Fisher. "That's standard with all magic-users."

"So we'll use the stone," said Hawk. "That's what it's for."

"Not so fast. If I was a sorcerer, I'd put a rider on my security spell, designed to go off if anybody messed with it."

Hawk frowned thoughtfully. "According to the Constable, Bode's a fairly low-level sorcerer. Something like that would need more sophisticated magic."

"Try the amulet again."

Hawk held the carved bone firmly in his hand, but it was still quiescent. As far as it was concerned, there wasn't any magic in the area. Hawk shook his head impatiently. "We're wasting time. We're going in there. Now."

"Fair enough."

"After you."

"My hero."

They walked slowly into the dim hallway, side by side. They paused just inside the doorway, but nothing happened. Hawk found a lamp in a niche on the wall, and lit it. The pale golden glow revealed a long narrow hallway, open but not particularly inviting. The walls were bare, the floor-boards dull and unpolished. There was a door to their right, closed, and a stairway straight ahead at the end of the hall. Fisher moved silently over to the door, listened a moment, and then eased it open. Hawk braced himself, axe at the

ready. Fisher pushed the door open with the toe of her boot
and stepped quickly into the room, sword held out before
her. Hawk moved quickly forward, holding up the lamp to
light the room. There was no one there. Everything looked
perfectly normal. Furniture, carpet, paintings and tapestries
on the walls. Nothing expensive, but comfortable. The two
Guards went back into the hall, shutting the door quietly
behind them. They headed for the stairs.

"Something's wrong here," said Hawk softly. "According to the amulet there's still no sign of any magic, but
this house should be saturated with it. At the very least,
there should be defensive spells all over the place. Indus-
trial espionage is rife among magic-users. There's always
someone trying to steal your secrets."

They made their way up the stairs, the steps occasionally
creaking under their weight. The sounds seemed very loud
on the quiet. The lamplight bobbed around them, unable
to make much impression on the darkness. The landing at
the top of the stairs led off onto a narrow hallway. There
were three doors, all firmly closed. Hawk and Fisher stood
together, listening, but there was only the quiet, and the
sound of their own breathing. Hawk sniffed at the air.

"Can you smell something, Isobel?"

"Yeah . . . something. Can't tell what it is, or where it's
coming from, though."

The nearest door suddenly flew open, slamming back
against the passageway wall with a deafening crash. Hawk
and Fisher moved quickly to stand on guard, weapons at
the ready. At first Hawk thought the figure before them was
some kind of beast, and it took him a moment to realise it
was a man wrapped in furs. He was barely average height,
but bulging with muscles, overdeveloped almost beyond
reason. His furs were dark and greasy, covered with filth
and dried blood. There was blood on his face and hands. He
was grinning widely, his cheeks stretched near to distortion.
Even so, Hawk had no trouble recognising the face Dr.
Jaeger had shown him in the pool of blood. The killer was
carrying something in his right hand, and Hawk darted a

glance at it. It was a severed head, held by the hair. Hawk
concentrated on the killer's face. The unnatural smile didn't
falter and the eyes were fixed and wild. His bearing was
savage and menacing, but he made no move to attack them.
Drugs? Possession? Crazy? Hawk took a firm hold on his
axe. He remembered what the killer had done to the body
in Silver Street with his bare hands.

"We're Captains in the city Guard," he said evenly.
"You're under arrest."

"You can't stop me," said the killer, his voice breathy
and excited. "I'm the Dark Man."

He swung the severed head viciously at Hawk, and he
stepped aside automatically. The head crashed into the wall
and rebounded, leaving a bloody smudge behind it. Fisher
stepped forward, her sword held out before her. The Dark
Man slapped the blade aside with the flat of his hand and
swung the severed head at her. She ducked, and the Dark
Man darted back into the room he'd come from. Hawk and
Fisher charged in after him, but the room was empty. Fisher
swore briefly.

"How the hell did he manage that? He was only out of
our sight for a second or two."

"Place is probably full of sliding panels and secret pas-
sageways," said Hawk. "He could be anywhere in the house
by now."

"Or out of it."

"No, I don't think so. We've seen his face. He has to
silence us, and he knows it. He'll be back. In the meantime,
let's take a look round these rooms. Maybe we'll find a clue,
or something to explain what's going on."

"Optimist," said Fisher.

The room they were in was a small, cosy bedchamber.
The bedclothes had been pulled back, but the bed was empty. The bedclothes felt cold and faintly damp to the touch.
There was a light covering of dust over all the furniture.
Hawk and Fisher poked around for a few minutes, but there
was nothing significant to be found. They went back out
into the hallway, keeping their weapons at the ready.

The next room turned out to be some kind of laboratory. There were glass instruments and tubing, earthenware bowls, and stacked phials of chemicals. The room looked neat and undisturbed, but once again there was a layer of dust over everything. At the back of the room there was a simple desk with two locked drawers. Fisher opened them. Inside there was nothing but a handful of papers, covered with complex equations that made no sense to either of them. Hawk put them back, and then paused and sniffed the air. The smell seemed somewhat stronger, and he had an uncomfortable suspicion he knew what it was.

The third and last room was a study. Small, compact, and tidy. Bookshelves covered one wall, packed with leather-bound volumes of varying sizes. There was a broad, functional desk, its top covered with scattered papers. The smell of death and decay was very strong. Posed limply in the chair by the desk was a dead man dressed in sorcerer's black. He'd been dead for some time. His head was bowed forward, his chin resting on his chest.

"Well, at least now we know what happened to the sorcerer Bode," said Fisher. "And why there's no magic in this place. His protective spells must have collapsed when he died."

"I don't think so," said Hawk. "Protective spells don't work like that."

"They couldn't have been very good spells. They didn't keep the killer out."

"Yes," said Hawk. "Interesting, that."

"So, how did he die?"

"Good question," said Hawk. "There's no obvious wound." He put the lamp down on the desk, gingerly took hold of the sorcerer's hair, and tilted the head back. When he saw Bode's face he almost let it drop forward again. The sorcerer had the same face as the Dark Man.

"That's not possible," said Fisher. "It can't be him. This man's been dead for days."

Hawk nodded, and let the head fall forward again. "So

what did we just fight? A ghost?" He started to wipe his fingers on his cape, and then stopped as he realised what he'd just said. They looked at each other for a moment.

"This house is supposed to be haunted," said Fisher.

"Ghosts don't usually try to bash your brains out with a severed head," said Hawk firmly. "Not unless it's their own. And they're not usually built like weightlifters, either." He looked back at the body as a thought struck him. "Relax, Isobel. This definitely isn't the Dark Man. The build's all wrong. This guy's about as well-developed as a sparrow. I've seen more muscles on a Leech Street whore."

"The face is still the same, though," said Fisher. "Maybe they're brothers. Twins."

Hawk frowned. "Too obvious. Nothing's ever simple, where magic-users are concerned."

He leant forward, and steeling himself against the smell, he searched the body carefully for the cause of death. It didn't take him long. There was a narrow puncture wound just under the sternum. Someone had stabbed Bode through the heart. Hawk readjusted the sorcerer's clothing, stood back, and frowned thoughtfully. One thrust, right through the heart. Very professional. Or very lucky. But even so, how had the killer got close enough to do it? Even a low-level sorcerer like Bode should have had more than enough magic to deal with a common assassin. Even assuming the killer had somehow got past the house's magical defences. Bode had to have had some defences, or a rival sorcerer would have wiped him out by now. Sorcery was a very competitive business. Particularly in the Northside.

Maybe Bode knew his killer, and invited him in. That would explain a lot. Including why the sorcerer had died sitting quietly in his own study.

"Hawk," said Fisher suddenly, "I think you'd better take a look at this."

Hawk looked round. Fisher had been studying the papers on the desk and was flipping through half a dozen sheets, frowning intently. He moved over to join her.

"Most of this is routine," said Fisher. "Reports on experiments, memos to himself not to forget things, dates and addresses and stuff like that. But this is . . . something else."

Hawk listened intently as Fisher read the pages aloud. It seemed Bode had to travel a lot, to acquire certain ingredients for his experiments. Which meant leaving his house unguarded, apart from the few magical defences he'd been able to put together. Bode was a better alchemist than sorcerer, and he knew his defences wouldn't keep out any really determined sorcerer. Being more than a little paranoid where his work was concerned, he put a lot of thought into protecting his home while he was away. He did think briefly about acquiring a familiar of some kind, but that meant dealing with some very unpleasant Beings, most of which were well out of his league. So he made his own familiar. He used his knowledge of sorcery and alchemy to reach inside himself, extract all the hate and rage and violence, and place them inside a homunculus; a sorcerously created duplicate of himself. The Dark Man. The familiar was bound to the house, and couldn't leave without Bode's permission. It made an excellent watchdog.

Fisher stopped reading, and looked at Hawk. "Like you said, the Northside brings out the worst in people."

"It does explain a lot," said Hawk. "Presumably the Dark Man was out of the house when Bode was killed, and it's been running loose ever since. Hating and killing because that's all it was ever designed to do. And now there's nothing left to hold it in check."

"We're going to have to kill it, Hawk," said Fisher. "We can't reason with something like this."

"We've got to find it first. Or wait for it to find us. Dammit, what was a low-level sorcerer like Bode doing, messing around with homunculi? Those things are strictly illegal."

Fisher looked at him. "This is Haven, remember?"

"This stuff is heavy, even for the Northside. The creation of a homunculus carries a mandatory death penalty, if they catch you. Research into making homunculi has been banned for centuries. In some places they still hang, draw, and quarter people just for owning books that mention the damn things."

Fisher frowned. "What's so important about homunculi?"

"Like a great many other things, it all comes down to inheritance and bloodlines. How are you going to keep the Family bloodlines pure, if exact physical duplicates keep popping up all over the place? Homunculi make a mockery of inheritance laws. On top of that, there's always the possibility of someone important being murdered and then replaced by a duplicate. Not to mention how easy it would be for some sorcerer to create his own army of homunculi, and hire it out to anyone with a grudge against the established order."

"You've been reading up on this, haven't you?" said Fisher.

"It wouldn't do you any harm to spend a little time in the Guard library. You'd be surprised at some of the stuff they've got there."

"Can we get back to Bode's murder?" said Fisher. "These notes aren't just about his research, you know. I saved the best for last. Take a look at this."

She handed Hawk a sheaf of letters from the desk. He looked quickly through them, his frown gradually deepening. Someone had hired Bode to investigate something to do with the Street of Gods. The details had been left deliberately vague, as though the writer hadn't wanted to commit anything incriminating to paper. Presumably he and the sorcerer had known what they were talking about, at any rate.

"Whatever Bode found out, someone didn't want him passing it on," said Fisher.

"This is crazy," said Hawk. "What was a low-level sorcerer like Bode doing, messing about on the Street of Gods? They'd have eaten him alive. Literally, in some cases." Hawk shook his head slowly. "I'm starting to get a really bad feeling about this case, Isobel."

"You always say that at the beginning of a case, Hawk."

"And I'm usually right."

"That's Haven for you."

The door behind them flew open, and the Dark Man filled the doorway. Hawk and Fisher spun to face him, weapons at the ready. The Dark Man's hand snapped forward, and the severed head flew through the air and struck Hawk on the forehead. Hawk had a brief glimpse of the staring eyes and gaping mouth and then he was staggering backwards, pain blinding him, his thoughts vague and muzzy. Fisher quickly stepped forward to stand between him and the Dark Man. She kicked at the head, and it rolled away across the floor. The Dark Man charged forward, and Fisher thrust at him with her sword. He dodged the blade with inhuman speed, darted inside her reach, and grabbed her by the arm. She struck at him with her fist, but he didn't even notice. He threw her against the wall with sickening force, driving the breath out of her. She started to slide down the wall, but the Dark Man grabbed her by the throat with one hand and lifted her into the air. Her feet kicked helplessly inches above the floor. He was still smiling. And then Hawk stepped forward, swinging his axe double-handed, and buried it in the Dark Man's side.

Ribs splintered and broke under the heavy blade, and the Dark Man staggered to one side, dropping Fisher to the floor. Hawk jerked his blade free, and blood flew on the air. He and the Dark Man stood facing each other for a moment, each judging the other's condition. The Dark Man was bleeding freely, but otherwise showed no weakness from his wound. Hawk had a huge bruise forming on his forehead, and his hands weren't as steady as he would have liked. The Dark Man's smile widened slightly, and he threw himself at Hawk, hands reaching like claws for Hawk's throat. Hawk buried his axe deep in the Dark Man's chest, but he just kept coming.

And then he froze suddenly, and all the hate and savagery went out of his face, to be replaced by something like surprise. He turned his head slowly to look at Fisher, who was leaning against the wall, and then he fell forward onto his face and lay still. Hawk looked at Fisher. The suppressor stone was glowing brightly in her hand like a miniature star. Hawk grinned at her.

"Told you it would come in handy."

He leant over the Dark Man and pulled his axe free. Fisher came over to join him, and they leaned on each other for a moment.

"I should have worked it out before," said Fisher. "If he was an homunculus, he was a magical construct. The suppressor stone took away his magic, and there was nothing left to hold him together."

Hawk nodded slowly. "I'm going to have to pay more attention to morning briefings."

2

The God Squad

Hawk and Fisher were snatching a late breakfast at a fast-food stall when the sound of a struck gong filled their minds, followed by the dry acid voice of the Guard communications sorcerer. Hawk nearly choked on his mouthful of sausage, and Fisher burnt her tongue on the mustard.

Captains Hawk and Fisher, you are to report to the Deity Division on the Street of Gods. Your orders are waiting for you there. You are seconded to the Division until further notice. Message ends.

The rasping voice was suddenly gone from their minds. Hawk spat out his mouthful of sausage, and shook his head gingerly. "If he doesn't stop using that bloody gong I swear I'm going to pay him a visit and stick it somewhere painful."

Fisher snorted. "From what I hear, you'd have to join the queue. This would have to happen now, right in the middle of a murder case. The Deity Division; what the hell does the God Squad want with us?"

"Beats me," said Hawk. "Maybe a God's got out of hand, and they want us to lean on him."

Fisher looked at him. "I hope you're not going to talk like that on the Street of Gods, Hawk. Because if you are, I'd be obliged if you'd keep well away from me. As I understand it, most Gods don't have a sense of humour. And the few

that do have a downright nasty one. After all, we're talking about Beings who tend towards striking down heretics
with lightning bolts, and dispensing plagues of boils when
Church takings are down on the week before."

"You worry too much," said Hawk.

"And it's all because of you," said Fisher.

The Street of Gods lies in the centre of Haven, right in the
middle of the high-rent district. Hundreds of religions crowd
side by side up and down the Street, promising hope and
salvation, doom and destruction, and whatever else people
need to keep them from thinking about the darkness at the
end of all life. Everyone needs something to believe in,
something that offers comfort in the face of despair, and
whatever it is you're looking for, you'll find it somewhere
on the Street of Gods. Churches and temples of all kinds
stand shoulder to shoulder, each proclaiming the glory of its
particular God and ostentatiously ignoring everyone else's.
Everywhere you look there's a High Priest claiming to know
the Truth of All Existence, and ready to share it with the
faithful in return for regular tithes and offerings. Religion
is big business in Haven.

According to the official city maps, the Street of Gods
is exactly half a mile long. In fact, the Street is as long as
it has to be to fit everything in. It's possible to start at one
end of the Street, walk all day, and still not reach the far
end before night falls. And then there are always the little
side streets and back alleys, unmarked on any map, where
the persistent enquirer can find the more controversial faiths
and religions, the existence of which is often hotly denied in
the clear light of day. There are doors that lead to mysteries,
to wonders and nightmares, and few of them can be found
in the same place twice.

Reality tends to be rather elastic on the Street of Gods.

The Deity Division, commonly known as the God Squad,
exists to keep order on the Street. The city Council appoints
its members, pays its wages, and does its best to pretend the
Squad doesn't exist. Most of the time they try to pretend the
whole damned Street doesn't exist. It makes them nervous.

On the whole, things tend to be quiet on the Street. The great majority of Beings prefer to believe they're the only ones there, and won't even admit the existence of any other Churches. But there are always the occasional feuds and vendettas, human and inhuman natures being what they are. The God Squad was there to try and head off confrontations before they happened, whenever possible. Sometimes it wasn't possible, and that was when the Squad earned their money.

"You worked with the Squad once, didn't you?" said Hawk to Fisher, as they made their way through the slush-covered streets towards the heart of the city. The sun was starting its slow climb up the sky, and the freezing streets were full of well-wrapped people heading to and from work.

"Briefly," said Fisher. "It was while you were working on that werewolf case, the one where young Hightower died. I was teamed with five other Guards on the Shattered Bullion case, and we spent a few days working with the God Squad. Didn't come to anything."

"What were they like?" said Hawk.

Fisher shrugged. "Stuck-up bunch, as I recall."

"Apart from that, what were they like? Give me some details, Isobel. Like it or not, we've got to work with these people, and I want to know what I'm getting into."

Fisher scowled thoughtfully. "The Squad is always made up of three people: a sorcerer, a mystic, and a warrior. Individuals come and go, but the mix stays the same. Presumably the Council are so relieved at finally finding a balance that works, they don't want to mess with it. This particular group has been together for four years. They've got a good track record.

"The sorcerer is called Tomb. Cheerful name. He's a bit older than us, quiet, thoughtful, powerful as all hell, and so easygoing it's disgusting. One of those people who prides himself on never raising his voice. A pigeon could crap on his head and he wouldn't ask for a handkerchief. Probably have ulcers by the time he's forty.

"The mystic is called Rowan. She's young, a pleasant enough sort, but crazy as a brewery-rat. Heavily into signs and omens and herbalistic remedies. She gave me a herb tea for my head cold, and I had the runs for two days. She's got the Sight, and a few minor magics, but mostly she earns her keep by figuring out how the various Beings think. She's supposed to be very good at that. Probably because she's just as weird as they are.

"The warrior is Charles Buchan. You must have heard of him. The greatest duelist, intriguer, and womanizer this city's ever known. Mid-forties, handsome, daring, and debonair—and about as modest as a peacock. Been getting into scrapes all his life, and talking and fighting his way out of them with equal ease. But he really shouldn't have sneaked past the King's Guards and gone to bed with the King's latest mistress on the same night the King decided to pay her a visit.

"Apparently he was given a straight choice: a career in the Guard or a lifetime in gaol. How he ended up in the God Squad is anybody's guess, but he's taken to it like a politician to bribes."

"And this is the group we're joining," said Hawk. "Great. Just great. I'm going to hate this assignment; I just know it. I was looking forward to working on the dead sorcerer case. How is it that whenever there's a particularly dangerous or unpleasant job that needs doing, our names are always at the top of the list?"

"Because we're the best," said Fisher. "And because we're too honest for our own good. The odds are we were getting too close to something sensitive, and someone wanted us out of the way for a while."

"Someone among our own superiors in the Guard."

"Probably. That's Haven for you."

Hawk growled something indistinct under his breath.

They came finally to the Street of Gods and stepped suddenly out of winter and into summer. The snow and slush stopped dead at the entrance to the Street, and the air was dry and warm. A bright midday sun shone overhead in a clear blue sky. Hawk looked at Fisher, but neither of them said anything. The Street of Gods went its own way and followed its own rules. Whatever they were.

Hawk and Fisher made their way down the Street, staring resolutely straight ahead. They'd visited the Street before, while working on their last case, and knew how easy it was to get distracted. Crowds of priests and worshippers bustled back and forth on unknown errands, and the air was full of the clamour of the street preachers, spreading the Word to anyone who would listen. A huge shadow plunged the Street into gloom for a moment as something impossibly massive passed by overhead. Hawk didn't look up. Whatever it was, he didn't want to know. The shadow passed on, and the bright sunlight returned. Hawk began to sweat heavily under his furs and cloak.

Something like a man-sized toad squatted on a street corner and sang sweetly with a young girl's voice. The begging bowl before it was filled with bloody pieces of meat. Something long and spindly with too many legs scuttled up the side of a building, hugging a dead cat to its thorax. A small child with ancient eyes thrust steel pins through its own arms, giggling obscenely. A street preacher was levitating three or four feet above the ground, his head hanging back, his face a mask of ecstasy. Only the tourists paid any attention. It took more than mere exhibitionism to attract a following on the Street of Gods.

The God Squad's headquarters turned out to be a squat little two-storey building tucked away in one of the many quiet backwaters off the Street of Gods. Hawk knocked twice on the discreet front door, and then he and Fisher waited patiently on the front step, keeping a watchful eye on the area, just in case. The narrow back alley seemed calm and quiet, but Hawk wasn't ready to take anything on trust in the Street of Gods. The door finally opened, revealing a short bald man in his early thirties, dressed in sorcerer's black. He beamed at the two Guards like a benevolent uncle, and it took Hawk a moment to realise that this pleasant-looking fellow had to be the sorcerer Tomb.

"Captain Fisher, my dear. How nice to see you again. And you must be Captain Hawk. Delighted. Do come in, do come in. We've been expecting you."

He ushered the two Guards down a short passage and into a small but comfortably appointed drawing room. He fussed around them as they settled into their chairs, keeping up a pleasant chatter all the while. Hawk took all of this with a pinch of salt. Tomb might like to come across as everyone's favourite relative, but you didn't get to be a first-class sorcerer through good intentions and a charming personality. It took long years of single-minded dedication, and not a little ruthlessness. Hawk smiled politely at Tomb's jokes, and made a mental note not to turn his back on the sorcerer. He didn't trust people who smiled too much. Tomb finally produced an exquisite cut-glass decanter and poured three generous glasses of sherry. Hawk took his and sipped it perfunctorily. He'd never much cared for the syrupy stuff, but he knew Fisher loved it. Tomb stopped talking for a moment as he savoured his sherry, and Hawk took advantage of the pause to get in a few words of his own.

"Pardon me, sir Tomb, but perhaps you could inform us as to what we're doing here. Usually when the God Squad needs help, you call in the Special Wizardry And Tactics team. What good can a couple of ordinary Guards do you?"

Tomb bit his lower lip and looked suddenly furtive. "If you don't mind, Captain Hawk, I think we ought to wait until both my colleagues are here. They won't be long. The situation is . . . rather complicated."

The door suddenly flew open, and Hawk and Fisher looked round, startled, as a stocky young woman strode in, slamming the door shut behind her. She stood glaring at Hawk and Fisher for a long moment, nose in the air and hands on hips. She was short, barely five feet in height, which made her look even heavier than she was, and her round, pleasant face was marred by a perpetual scowl. Her dark hair was cropped short like a helmet, and her heavy eyebrows intensified her fierce demeanour. The dark, shapeless robe she wore was more suited to an older woman. She couldn't have been much into her twenties, but she looked at least ten years older.

"What are they doing here?" she snapped, switching her glare to the sorcerer Tomb. "I told you I didn't want them here."

"The Council sent them," said Tomb easily, apparently unaffected by her angry stare. "They seem to think we could do with a little help."

The woman sniffed loudly. "If we can't work out what the hell's going on with all our experience, I don't see how a couple of strong-arm bullies from the Guard are going to help."

"That's enough, Rowan," said Tomb sharply, and there was enough bite in his tone to silence the mystic.

Hawk studied Tomb thoughtfully over his sherry glass. It would seem the sorcerer had hidden depths after all. Hawk was just nerving himself to try another sip of his sherry, when the door flew open again and a tall muscular man strode in, shoulders back, head held high. Hawk didn't need Fisher to tell him that this was the notorious Charles Buchan.

He was handsome in a harsh, brooding way, with a head of close-cropped blond curls and icy blue eyes, and his arms and chest showed the kind of muscle definition you only get from lifting weights. He was supposed to be in his forties, but his superb physique made him look a good ten years younger. He was dressed in the latest fashion and wore it well, which took some doing when you considered that the latest style consisted of tightly cut trousers and a padded jerkin with a chin-high collar. In fact, if the trousers had been cut any more tightly, Hawk would have seriously considered arresting the man for indecent exposure. Buchan's clothes were brightly colored but stopped just short of being garish; so short that the effect had to be intentional. Hawk couldn't help noticing that the outfit had been carefully tailored so that there was plenty of give around the chest and shoulders. Charles Buchan might like to look up-to-the-minute, but clearly he wasn't prepared to let that interfere with his fighting abilities.

Hawk shot a glance at Fisher to see what she made of the man, and was disturbed to find her studying Buchan with a smile on her face. Hawk's eyebrows had just started to descend into a scowl, when Buchan stepped forward and greeted him cheerfully, slapping him just a little too hard on the shoulder. Hawk winced despite himself. Buchan turned to Fisher, who extended a hand to him. He took her hand, raised it to his lips, and kissed it expertly, his eyes on hers. Hawk's scowl deepened. Fisher didn't normally let people kiss her hand. Buchan let go of her hand with becoming reluctance, and straightened up to his full height, pulling back his shoulders a little so as to show off his broad chest and flat stomach.

"So, this is the famous partnership of Hawk and Fisher. I've heard a lot about you, all of it good. Glad to have you with us on this case. I'm sure it's going to be fascinating working with you. But I'm afraid there isn't that much for you to do, actually. I've no doubt we'll solve this case soon enough. We always do, you know. Still, I'm sure we can find something to keep you occupied while you're here."

His voice was deep, resonant and commanding. *It would be*, thought Hawk dourly. *I'll bet he smokes a pipe as well, and cracks nuts with his bare hands. A devil with the ladies and a natural leader of men. Given a few spare minutes, I think I could learn to hate this guy.*

"Indeed," said Tomb. "If you don't mind, Charles, I'd like to take this opportunity to explain to our new friends why they're here."

"Of course," said Buchan. "Don't mind me. Go straight ahead."

He leaned back against the doorway, took a pipe from his pocket and began cleaning it, whistling softly under his breath. There was a pause, as everyone looked at Tomb. He frowned slightly, as though uncertain where to start.

"We find ourselves in a rather unusual situation, Captain Hawk, Captain Fisher. My associates and I have worked on many strange cases in our time in the Squad, but I have to say we've never encountered anything quite like this. To put it bluntly, someone is killing the Gods of Haven."

Hawk and Fisher looked at each other. "Go on," said Hawk.

"We've lost three Beings so far," said Tomb. "The Dread Lord, the Sundered Man, and the Carmadine Stalker. We don't know how they died, or why, but all three have been utterly destroyed. If we don't come up with some explanations soon, the Gods are going to panic, and the Street of Gods could end up as a battleground. There are a lot of old grudges among the Gods, and it wouldn't take much to set them at each other's throats."

"I didn't think Gods could die," said Fisher.

"Call them Beings, if it will help," said the mystic Rowan. "If you're to be of any help to us, you have to understand how the Street of Gods operates. There are all kinds of religion here—some old, some new, some just fashions of the moment. Most are based around supernatural entities who've gathered a following through displays of power and promises of worldly dominion. Everyone wants to be on the winning side, to have a powerful protector watching out for them. Then there are human preachers whose teachings have developed into a religion. Their Churches tend to last the longest. Ideas are much more powerful and enduring than some magical Being with an ego problem.

"Religions come and go, and we try to keep the peace. Some of them are strange, some of them are beautiful, and some we don't understand at all. People can believe in the weirdest things if they're frightened or desperate enough. We don't take sides. We just try to keep the feuds and vendettas under control, and make sure that whatever troubles there may be don't pass beyond the Street of Gods."

"How do you do that?" said Hawk.

The sorcerer Tomb smiled. "Talking things through, playing off one faction against another, and a lot of improvising. If things start to get too out of hand, we call in the SWAT team. If that fails, we turn to the Exorcist Stone. That's our last resort. Essentially it's a much more powerful version of the suppressor stone the Council's been experimenting with. The Exorcist Stone dispels all magic from an area, no matter how powerful, and can even banish a Being from this plane of existence."

"Banish?" said Fisher. "You mean destroy?"

The sorcerer shrugged. "We don't know. They disappear and they don't come back. We settle for that. We use the Stone very sparingly; only when there's a threat to the whole city. If the Beings decided we were a threat to them, they'd band together and destroy us. Stone or no Stone."

"Is that how the Gods have been dying?" said Hawk. "Someone's got hold of an Exorcist Stone of their own?"

"That's impossible," said Rowan flatly. "There's only one Stone, and no one knows how old it is or how it was created. If by chance there was another, we'd know about it. Every magic-user for hundreds of miles around would know about it; the sheer power involved would blaze like a beacon in their mind's eye. No one but the three of us has access to the Exorcist Stone, and it's impossible for any of us to misuse it. When we join the God Squad, the Council places a geas on us, a spell of compulsion, to prevent any of us using the Exorcist Stone except in the line of duty."

"But still the Gods keep dying," said Buchan. "Their bodies destroyed, their presence dispersed. We've tried to investigate, but we have no experience in such matters. We've got nowhere. We don't even know what to look for. So far, the Gods' followers are still in shock; too dazed to do anything but sit around and pray for their Gods to return. When that doesn't happen, they're going to get angry and start looking for scapegoats."

"And if that wasn't bad enough," said Tomb, "we're starting to hear rumblings from the other Beings. The three unexplained deaths have left them feeling vulnerable and afraid. It's only a matter of time before they decide to take matters into their own hands. We could end up with a God War on the Street. I don't think Haven could survive such a war. I'm not even sure the Low Kingdoms would survive."

"So we sent to the Council for help," said Buchan. "And they sent us you."

"The notorious Hawk and Fisher," said Rowan, her voice flat and scathing. "A pair of thugs in uniform. I know all about your reputation. You're the most violent Guards in Haven. You don't care who you hurt. No one knows how many people you've killed."

"You should visit the Northside," said Hawk. "It might open your eyes to a few things. Northsiders don't believe in reasoned argument or diplomacy. They tend more to poisoning your wine or slipping a dagger between your ribs. Or both. We have the highest murder rate, the worst violence, and the highest general crime rate in all Haven. We're only as hard as we have to be, to get results. That's all the Council cares about."

"That's as may be," said Tomb weightily, "But I feel it only fair to warn you that I won't tolerate such strong-arm tactics here. They'd just get you killed; you and anyone else unfortunate enough to be with you at the time. I must insist that while you're a part of the Squad you follow my orders at all times. Is that clear?"

"Sure," said Fisher.

"Of course," said Hawk.

Tomb looked at them both suspiciously. He'd expected to have to argue the point, and their giving in so easily worried him. It wasn't in character. He pursed his lips and decided to let it pass, for the moment. "There is one other thing we need to discuss," he said slowly. "What religion do you both follow? What do you believe in?"

"Death and taxes," said Fisher promptly. "Everything else is negotiable."

"Isobel and I were both raised as Christians," said Hawk quickly, to deflect Tomb's deepening scowl. "I've seen a lot of darkness in my time, but I still trust in the light."

"Christianity," said Tomb thoughtfully. "The Old Religion. You're from the Northern countries originally, I take it? Yes, I thought so. I'm afraid your religion isn't much practised in the Low Kingdoms, though of course many of its terms still survive in the language. We really must sit down and discuss this some day."

"Christians," said Rowan disdainfully. "I thought you people believed in love and peace, and turning the other cheek?"

"We're not very orthodox," said Hawk.

"Well, just remember you're only here on sufferance." Rowan sniffed disgustedly. "All the Guards we could have had, and they had to send us a pair of Christians."

"Apparently you have a friend on the Council," said Buchan.

"Councillor Adamant, to be exact," said Tomb. "I understand you behaved very creditably while working as his bodyguards during the election. Though why he thinks that should qualify you to work on the Street of Gods is beyond me."

"We fought a God on his behalf," said Hawk calmly. "The Abomination, the Lord of the Gulfs. We helped kill it."

A sudden silence fell across the room. The three members of the God Squad looked at Hawk and Fisher almost respectfully.

"That was you?" said Buchan.

"We had some help," said Hawk. Fisher's mouth twitched.

"I don't believe it," said Rowan flatly.

Hawk looked at her calmly. "That's your problem, lass." He turned away to look at Tomb and Buchan. "Fisher and I aren't exactly strangers to the Street of Gods. We've been here before. And whilst we might not have much experience in dealing with Beings, we do know how to track down murderers. That's our job. We're very good at it."

Rowan started to say something scathing, and then stopped suddenly and looked at Tomb. "People are gathering out on the Street. They seem angry, disturbed. I don't like the feel of it, Tomb."

The sorcerer nodded slowly. "I can See them, Rowan. Two large factions, closing on each other. Damn. There's going to be another riot. Charles, Rowan. Gather your equipment. Hawk and Fisher, come with me. You're about to see what happens when the rules break down on the Street of Gods. You should find it an interesting experience. If you survive it."

Out on the Street of Gods, everything felt different. There was a vague unfocused tension on the air, and the crowding buildings felt grim and oppressive. Hawk and Fisher hurried along beside the God Squad, weapons drawn and at the ready. Tomb took the point, striding confidently in the lead, his robe of sorcerer's black billowing impressively around his stocky frame. He was smiling calmly, his stance relaxed and at ease.

Rowan hurried along at his side, stretching her legs to keep up with him. She carried a bulging satchel on one shoulder, and her face had taken on an uncomplicated expression of bulldog determination. Away from Tomb's comfortable study, she looked stronger, more focused, almost elemental in her single-mindedness. Charles Buchan strolled along behind them, his long legs easily meeting their pace. He wore a brightly polished chain-mail vest, and a long sword on his left hip. He carried himself well, his bearing calm and controlled. His face was a smiling, pleasant mask, but his eyes were very cold.

Hawk kept a watchful eye on the Squad as they hurried down the Street of Gods. Even with their practised professionalism, he could all but see the tension rising off them. He started to wonder if he ought to feel more worried himself. After all, this was their territory; if they were worried, there was probably a damned good reason for it. The Street itself seemed increasingly uneasy. There were fewer people around than previously, and they hurried on their way with heads bowed and eyes downcast. The street preachers were crying of universal death and destruction. A painted clown with razor blades buried in his bleeding eyes sang a bitter song of love and loss. Two shadows with nothing to cast them tore at each other like maddened animals. A tall angular building began to melt and run away like boiling wax, while the gargoyles on its guttering screamed in agony.

Hawk increased his pace and moved in beside the sorcerer Tomb. "Pardon me, sir Tomb, but if my partner and I are heading into a dangerous situation, I think we have a right to know what we're getting into."

"Of course," said Tomb. "You'll have to forgive us, Captain, but I'm afraid we're not used to working with strangers. Rowan and I both have the Sight, the ability to see and sense things at a distance. It seems a longstanding rivalry between two religions has boiled over into open fighting on the Street. The way things are, if we don't put a stop to it quickly, it'll develop into a full-blown riot, and the Beings themselves may be tempted to get involved. Normally, things wouldn't get this bad this quickly, but with three dead Gods and the murderer still at large, tempers are running short."

"Wait a minute," said Hawk. "If things are that serious shouldn't we call in the SWAT team?"

"Oh, I don't think so," said Tomb. "It's only a riot. We can handle it."

"Famous last words," muttered Fisher behind them.

Hawk gave Tomb a hard look, but the sorcerer seemed perfectly serious. "All right," said Hawk, "Give me some background on this. You said two religions. Which religions?"

"They're based on two lesser Beings," said Tomb. "Neither of them especially powerful or important, but both with long-established followings. Dusk the Devourer is head of a no-frills nihilist cult. Everything is vile and awful, the world's going to be destroyed, and only the faithful will be saved and transported to a better world. I can't prove it, but I'm fairly sure Dusk itself is a manic-depressive.

"The other Being is the Chrysalis. It's a huge cocoon about twenty feet long. It's supposed to perform the occasional miracle, but I've never seen any. The Chrysalis' followers believe that eventually the cocoon will open and the

God within will emerge in all its glory to purge the world of evil. Whether it wants to be purged or not. They've been watching the cocoon for over four hundred years, but nothing's happened yet.

"Interestingly enough, each religion is the other's particular nemesis. Every God must have its Devil, though I've never been sure why. Good business, I suppose. Anyway, normally the two groups of followers content themselves with blazing sermons, veiled insults in the Street, and the occasional scuffle after the taverns have closed. But with things as they are, nothing's normal anymore. The Street of Gods is like a forest in a drought, waiting for a single spark to set everything alight."

Hawk nodded. "Either that, or they heard Fisher and I were coming and wanted to put on a good show to welcome us."

Rowan muttered something indistinct. It didn't sound complimentary.

They heard the riot before they actually saw it. From up ahead came a roar of massed voices, raised in rage and hatred, and darkened with that animal single-mindedness found only in crowds that are rapidly turning into mobs. Hawk fell back a pace to walk beside Fisher. If they were going into a fight, he wanted someone at his back he could trust. The roar grew louder and more savage as they approached a sharp corner. According to the official maps, the Street of Gods was perfectly straight, but in this, as in so many other ways, the Street of Gods went its own way. They rounded the corner, and there was the riot, spread out before them.

A hundred men and women milled back and forth across the Street, mouths turned down in angry snarls, their eyes wild and furious. They were screaming and shouting and shaking their fists, and glaring in all directions. Some had clubs or staves or lengths of steel chain, while others had bricks or stones. Already there was blood on the cobbles, and several people lay unmoving on the ground, trampled on unnoticed by the mob. The scent of violence was heavy on the air, ready to erupt at any moment.

Hawk came to a halt well short of the mob, and looked the situation over carefully. The setting couldn't have been worse. The Street at this point was long and narrow, with only a few exits. Even if he could persuade the mob to break up and disperse, getting it separated into smaller, more manageable groups was going to be difficult. Breaking up a mob was one thing; keeping them separated was what counted. There had to be somewhere for them to go. The size of the watching crowd worried him as well. There were hundreds of them, filling the Street all around. Presumably they followed other faiths, and were happy at the chance to see two of their rivals knocking the hell out of each other. Even the street preachers had given up trying to spread the Word, and were busying themselves taking bets from the onlookers.

Tomb had come to a halt not far away and was watching the mob narrowly, lips pursed thoughtfully. Rowan was kneeling beside him, ferreting through her satchel. Hawk leaned over to take a look at what she had in there, and then quickly retreated as she glared at him viciously. Buchan was standing close at hand, his arms folded across his mailed chest, staring majestically out over the mob. He looked as though he was only awaiting the word to step forward and generally beat heads together until everyone agreed to see reason. Hawk looked quickly at Fisher, and was relieved to see she didn't appear too impressed. She caught him looking at her, realised why, and grinned broadly. Hawk looked away, and pretended he hadn't noticed. He hefted his axe thoughtfully, and watched the mood of the mob grow worse. This was the God Squad's territory, and he didn't want to interfere, but somebody had better do something soon or there'd be brains spilled on the cobbles and a riot you'd need a small army to contain.

Rowan drew a pair of slender copper rods from her satchel and plunged them into the ground. They sank easily into the solid stone as though it were nothing more than wet mud. The mystic then drew a protective circle around herself and Tomb with blue chalk dust. Hawk frowned slightly as he realised he and Fisher and Buchan weren't included in the protection. Whatever Rowan and Tomb were up to, he hoped they were careful to aim it in the right direction. The mystic and the sorcerer then paused for a technical discussion. Hawk moved over a little to stand beside Buchan, who was still silently studying the mob.

"Who's winning, sir Buchan?"

"Hard to tell. Strategically speaking, this is a mess. There's no cooperation; it's every man for himself and Devil take the hindmost. Quite literally, I suppose, as far as they're concerned."

"How do you tell the two sides apart?"

"Blue robes are Chrysalis, grey robes are Dusk."

"Are we going to break this up or not?" said Fisher, moving over to join them. "I can't just stand around and watch; it's bad for my reputation."

"It's better not to butt in too early," said Buchan. "Let them work off some of their bile on each other first."

"You mean we're just supposed to stand by and let people die?" said Fisher, her face falling into an ominous scowl.

"It's for the best," said Buchan. He looked at her and smiled slightly. "You're new to the Street, my dear. We know what we're doing." He realised Fisher was still glaring at him, and stirred uncomfortably. "I suppose you've got a better way?"

"A riot's a riot," said Fisher. "Hawk and I have handled a few in our time. You may be an expert in your territory, sir Buchan, but we're not exactly amateurs in ours."

"Well, if we can't handle this one, you may just get a chance to show us your expertise," said Buchan, just a little coolly.

Tomb and Rowan suddenly stood together and raised their arms in the stance of summoning. The mystic began to sing, an eerie atonal chant that cut through the din of the riot like a knife. Fights broke up, and people stopped shouting to sway unsteadily on their feet and clutch at their heads. Tomb spoke a Word of Power, and the crowd split suddenly in two, the grey and blue robes separated by some unseen force that left them in two confused crowds on opposite sides of the Street. Hawk shifted uncomfortably from foot to foot, and shook his head to clear it. The magic had only touched him briefly in passing, but he could appreciate how it must feel to those unfortunate enough to have suffered it full blast.

Rowan stopped singing, and the Street of Gods was suddenly quiet. The two crowds took their hands away from their heads and looked uncertainly around them. They spotted the God Squad, and a low rebellious murmur began, only to stop short as Buchan strode briskly forward into the middle of the Street. Hawk and Fisher looked at each other and then strode quickly after him. Whatever was going to happen next, they were determined not to be left out of it. Buchan took up a position between the two crowds, looked left and right, and then beckoned imperiously. There was a pause, and then two men came forward, one from each side. Each man's robe was the color of his faction, one grey and one blue, but these were gorgeously styled and decorated. From their haughty expressions and bearing, and the amount of jewellery they were wearing, Hawk decided these had to be the respective High Priests of Dusk and the Chrysalis. They came to a halt before Buchan, and bowed very slightly to him, each carefully ignoring the other.

"All right," said Buchan, "Who started it this time?"

For a moment, Hawk thought the two priests were going to point at each other and shout "He did!" like two children caught squabbling in the playground, but the moment passed. Both High Priests drew themselves up to their full height and glared at Buchan.

"Sir Field, sir Stoner," said Buchan, looking from the grey robe to the blue and back again, "I'm waiting for an answer."

"Dusk the Devourer has been insulted," said Field flatly.

"Dusk insults the Chrysalis by its very existence!" snapped Stoner.

"Blasphemer!"

"Heretic!"

"Liar!"

"Fraud!"

"That's enough!" said Buchan sharply, his hand dropping to the sword at his side.

The two priests quieted reluctantly, and turned their glares on Buchan rather than each other. Hawk frowned slightly. The High Priests were tense, but not cowed. They had their followers watching and neither of them was going to be the first to back down.

"I want you both to go back to your people and get them off the Street," said Buchan. "You know the rules. Disturbances like this are bad for business."

"To hell with your rules and to hell with your Squad," said Field. "Cast your spells and be damned. The Lord Dusk will protect his children."

"Your sorcerer and mystic can chant spells till they're blue in the face," said Stoner. "You won't take us by surprise again. We have our own magic-users."

Field nodded unflinchingly. "You're not in charge any more, Buchan. The Gods are dying and you've done nothing. From now on we defend ourselves."

Buchan just stood there, taken aback at being so openly defied, and the silence lengthened ominously.

Hawk glanced at Fisher. "You take blue, I'll take grey," he said briskly, and stepped forward axe in hand to face the High Priest of Dusk the Devourer. Field looked at him warily, but held his ground. Hawk grinned unpleasantly. "I'm Hawk, Captain in the city Guard. That's my partner, Captain Fisher. You may have heard of us. It's all true. Now get yourself and your people off the Street or I'll cut you off at the knees."

It was Field's turn to look taken aback, but he recovered more quickly than Buchan. "Lay a hand on me, Guard, and my followers will tear you apart."

"Maybe," said Hawk. "But you'll still be dead."

"You're bluffing."

"Try me."

Field met Hawk's unwavering gaze, and some of the confidence went out of him. A cold breeze touched the back of his neck as he realised the Guard meant exactly what he said. He looked over at Stoner, who was staring at Fisher like a rat mesmerized by a snake. Field looked back at Hawk and nodded slowly. He turned away to face his followers, careful to make no sudden movements that might upset the Guard. Talking slowly and calmly, he told his people the time was not yet right for direct confrontation and they should return to their homes and pray for guidance. Not far away, Stoner was putting the same message across to his people. The crowds stirred and muttered reluctantly, but eventually did as they were told. Field and Stoner turned back reluctantly to face Hawk and Fisher again.

"Very nicely done," said Hawk. "Now get the hell out of here. And if there's any more trouble, we'll know it's you, and we'll come looking for you."

"Right," said Fisher.

The two High Priests left with what dignity they could muster. Which wasn't much. Hawk looked at Buchan.

"A riot's a riot, sir Buchan. All you have to do is separate out the leaders, and break their authority."

"You were lucky," said Buchan tightly. "Real fanatics would have died rather than give in."

"But they weren't real fanatics," said Hawk. "I could tell."

"What would you have done if they had turned out to be the real thing?"

Hawk grinned. "Run like fun and screamed for the SWAT team. I'm not crazy."

"Right," said Fisher.

3

Gods and Devils
and Other Beings

The sorcerer Tomb led Hawk and Fisher down the Street of Gods, and the crowds parted before them to give them room. Curious eyes watched the Guards pass, but no one wanted to get too close. Word of their arrival on the Street had preceded them. Hawk and Fisher nodded politely to the few brave souls who ventured a greeting, and kept their eyes open for unfriendly faces. Their encounter with the High Priests hadn't made them any friends. And besides, for no reason he could put his finger on, Hawk felt more than usually uneasy about his surroundings. The Street of Gods had changed since the last time he saw it. The buildings pressed more closely together, as though for comfort and support, and the occasional creatures and manifestations had a dangerous, openly threatening air. Even the street preachers seemed wilder, more intent on messages of destruction and damnation. The Street had grown darker, colder, more turned in upon itself. As though it wasn't sure who it could trust anymore. Hawk looked at Fisher to see if she'd noticed the changes, and saw that her hand was back resting on the pommel of her sword. Fisher liked to be prepared.

The last time they'd visited the Street of Gods, Hawk and Fisher had been acting as bodyguards for the political candidate James Adamant, as he made the rounds of sympathetic Beings, looking for support in the elections. Adamant was now Councillor Adamant, though of course that didn't necessarily prove anything. One way or the other. But though even then the Street of Gods had been a strange and eerie place, with its creatures and illusions and uncertain reality, the Street that Hawk walked now seemed somehow more sour, and more defensive. As though it was on its guard . . . Hawk frowned. Presumably even Gods could get scared, with a God killer on the loose.

Hawk scowled, and let his hand fall to the axe at his side. More and more, he was feeling very much out of his depth. He'd faced some strange things in his time, but his experience in Haven was for the most part with human killers, with their everyday schemes and passions and hatreds. He knew how to handle them. But, for better or worse, he was stuck with the God Squad now, until either he found the killer or his superiors relented. He'd just have to get used to the Street, that was all. He'd seen worse, in his time.

A group of monks came striding down the Street of Gods, arms swinging with military precision. Their robes hung loosely about them, the cowls pulled forward to hide their faces. Tomb moved to one side to let them pass, and Hawk and Fisher did the same. Anything could be dangerous on the Street of Gods, and it paid to be careful. The monks went by, looking neither left nor right. Tomb waited until they'd passed, and then continued on his way. Hawk and Fisher followed on behind.

They were on their way to look at the churches of the three murdered Beings. Rowan wasn't with them, because she wasn't feeling well. Apparently she'd been quite ill recently, and spent a lot of time in bed, dosing herself with her herbal remedies. Hawk just hoped it wasn't catching. And Buchan was off somewhere on business of his own. No one asked what. Buchan being Buchan, no one really wanted to know. Which left Tomb to act as their guide.

The first murder site was a huge, solid building right in the middle of the Street. The walls were made of great stone blocks, each of them as big as a man. The church was three stories high, with narrow slits for windows. There was only one door, made of solid oak, and reinforced with wide steel bands. Hawk studied the building thoughtfully as Tomb fumbled with his key ring. The place looked more like a fortress than a church. Which suggested this was a religion with enemies, in the Church's mind if nowhere else. And it had to be said that worship of the Dread Lord hadn't been an exactly popular religion. Human sacrifice wasn't banned on the street of Gods, as long as it didn't endanger the tourists, but it was frowned on. Tomb finally located the right key and unlocked the huge padlock affixed to the door. He pushed the door with his fingertips, and it swung silently open on its counterweights. Hawk studied the dark opening suspiciously.

"There's no one in there, Captain Hawk," said Tomb reassuringly. "After the murder was discovered I set up protective wards to keep out vandals and souvenir hunters, and they're still in place. No one's been here since I left. Follow me, please."

Tomb walked confidently into the gloom, and Hawk and Fisher followed him in, hands hovering over their weapons. A bright blue glow appeared around the sorcerer, pushing back the darkness and illuminating the hallway. The hall was grim and oppressive, without ornament or decoration of any kind. Tomb allowed them a few moments to look around, and then led them toward a door at the far end of the hall. The front door slammed shut behind them. Hawk jumped, but wouldn't give Tomb the satisfaction of looking back. The second door opened onto a rough wooden stairway, leading down into darkness.

"Watch the steps," said Tomb. "Some of them are slippery, and there's no handrail."

They followed the stairs down into the darkness for a long time. Hawk tried to keep count, but he kept losing track. By the time they reached the bottom, Hawk realised they had to be uncomfortably far beneath the city, down in the bedrock itself. Tomb gestured abruptly with his left hand,

and the bright blue glow flared up, shedding its light over a larger area. Hawk and Fisher looked wonderingly about them. The stairs had brought them to a vast stone chamber, hundreds of feet in diameter. The walls were rough and unfinished, but the sharp edges left by the original cutting tools had been mostly smoothed over by air and moisture in the many years since the cavern had been hewn from the living rock.

Stalactites and stalagmites hung down from the ceiling and jutted up from the cavern floor. There were pools of dark water, and thick white patches of fungi spattered across the walls. There were cobwebs everywhere, shrouding the walls and hanging in tatters between the stalactites and stalagmites. Fisher touched one strand with a fingertip, and it stretched unnaturally before it snapped. Fisher pulled a face, and wiped her hand clean on her cloak. It was very quiet, and the slightest echo seemed to linger uncomfortably before fading away into whispers. In the middle of the cavern, the webbing had thickened and come together to form a huge hammock, hanging suspended above their heads from the thickest stalactites. It was torn and tattered now, but there was enough left to suggest the immense size of the form that had once hung within it.

"Gods come in all shapes and sizes," said Tomb quietly. "They can be human or inhuman, both and neither. People don't seem to care much, provided they're promised the right things."

"You never did say what you believed in, sir Tomb," said Fisher.

Tomb smiled. "I'm not sure I believe in anything, anymore, my dear. Working on the Street of Gods will do that to you. It makes you doubt too many things. Or perhaps it just makes you cynical. We need Gods, all of us. They offer hope and comfort and forgiveness, and most of all they offer reassurance. We're all afraid of dying, afraid of going alone into the dark. And perhaps even more than that, we need to believe in something greater than ourselves, something to give our lives meaning and purpose."

"What happened to the body?" said Hawk. "I take it the Being did have a body?"

"Oh, yes, Captain Hawk. It's over there. What's left of it."

Tomb led them across the gloomy cavern to what Hawk had taken for an exceptionally large boulder. It turned out to be a huge pile of sharp-edged objects, dark and glazed, held together in one place by strands of webbing. It took Hawk a while to work out what he was looking at, but eventually some of the shapes took on sense and meaning, and his lip curled in disgust. Going by the size of the carapace segments and the many jointed legs, the Dread Lord had been more insect than anything else. The pile of broken pieces stood nearly ten feet tall, and was easily as broad. The Being itself must have been huge. Hawk shivered involuntarily. He'd never liked insects.

"Was it in pieces like this when you found it?" he said finally.

"More or less," said Tomb. "The pieces were strewn across the floor of the chamber. Whatever killed this Being tore the body apart as though it were nothing but paper. Its followers . . . tidied it up."

"So the killer has to be immensely strong," said Fisher. She thought for a moment, staring at the pile before her. "This . . . dismembering—Was it done while the Being was still alive, or after it was dead?"

"I don't know," said Tomb. "I hadn't really thought about it. How can you tell?"

"By the amount of blood," said Hawk. "It stops flowing after you're dead. So if there's not much blood splashed around a dismembered body, it's a safe enough bet the victim was dead at the time. You learn things like that in the Northside."

"I see," said Tomb. "Most interesting. But not much help here, I'm afraid. The Dread Lord didn't have any blood. Its body was hollow."

Hawk and Fisher looked at each other. "This case gets better all the time," said Fisher.

"Do we have any clues as to the motive?" said Hawk. "Did the Dread Lord have any particular enemies or rivals? Someone who might profit by its death?"

Tomb shook his head. "There was no feud or vendetta as far as we can tell. The Dread Lord hadn't been on the Street long enough to acquire that kind of enemy."

"All right," said Hawk patiently. "Let's try something simpler. Do we know when the murder took place?"

"Some time during the early hours of the morning, nine days ago. The High Priest came down to consult with his God about whatever nihilists consider important, and found his God scattered across the cavern floor."

"Can we question him about it?" said Fisher.

"Not easily," said Tomb. "The High Priest and all the Dread Lord's followers are dead. Suicide. That's nihilists for you."

"Great," said Hawk. "No witnesses to the murder, no clues at the scene of the crime, and no one left to question. I've only been on this case a few hours, and already it's driving me crazy. Nothing in this damned case makes sense. I mean, how did the killer get down here? I assume the church was well-guarded?"

"Oh, yes," said Tomb. "Over a hundred armed guards, supplied by the Brotherhood of Steel. No one saw anything."

"I hate this case," said Fisher.

"This is the Street of Gods, Captain Fisher. Normal rules and logic don't apply here."

Hawk looked at the pile of broken and splintered chitin that had once been worshipped as a God, shook his head slowly, and turned his back on it. "We're not going to learn anything useful here. I'll call in the forensic sorcerers, and see what they can turn up." He stopped. Tomb was shaking his head. "All right. What's wrong now?"

"I don't think the Beings would allow that kind of investigative sorcery on their territory. The Gods must have their mysteries."

"Even though the sorcerers might come up with something to keep them alive?"

"Even then."

"Damn. In that case, we'll just have to do it the hard way. Take us to the next murder site, sir Tomb. And let's hope we can dig up something useful there."

At first glance it was just an ordinary house. Two storeys, slate roof, good brickwork. Windows and brasswork had been recently cleaned. It looked as out of place on the Street of Gods as a lamb in a wolfpack. Tomb knocked politely on the door, and there was a long pause.

"Are you sure this is the right place?" said Fisher. "This is the closest I've ever seen to archetypal merchant-class housing. All it needs is a rococo boot-scraper and a lion's-head door-knocker and it'd be perfect. What kind of God would live here?"

"The Sundered Man," said Tomb. "And he doesn't live here anymore. He was murdered six days ago. Show some respect, Captain, please."

They waited some more. People passed by on the Street of Gods, going about their business in the warm Summer sun, but all of them seemed to have some kind of smile for the people waiting outside the tacky little two up, two down merchant's house. Fisher took to glaring indiscriminately at anyone who even looked in their direction.

"Are you sure there's somebody in there?" said Hawk.

"There's a caretaker," said Tomb. "Sister Anna. I contacted her earlier today, and she said she'd be here."

There was the sound of bolts being drawn back from inside, and they turned to face the door again. It swung suddenly open, revealing a plain-faced, average-looking woman in her late forties. She was dressed well but not expensively, in a style that had last been fashionable a good ten years ago. She looked tired and drawn, and somehow defeated by life. She smiled briefly at Hawk and Fisher, and bowed politely to Tomb.

"Good day, sir sorcerer, Captains. I'm sorry I took so long, but all the others have left now, and I have to do everything myself. Please, come in."

She stood back, and Tomb led the two Guards into the hall. It was just as narrow and gloomy as Hawk had expected, with bare floorboards and plain wood panelling on the walls. But everything was neat and tidy, and the simple furniture glowed from recent polishing. Sister Anna shut the door, and slid home four heavy bolts. She caught Hawk looking at her, and smiled self-consciously.

"Our God has been dead barely a week, and already the vultures are gathering on the Street. If sir Tomb hadn't put protective wards round the house on his first visit, they'd have torn the place apart by now, searching for objects of power and whatever loot they could lay their hands on. Not that they'd have found much of either. We were never a rich or powerful Order. We had our God, and his teachings, and that was all. It was enough. As it is, the memory of the wards keep most of them away, and the locks and bolts take care of the rest. This way, please."

She led them into a pleasant little drawing room, and saw them all comfortably seated before departing for the kitchen to get them some tea. Hawk slipped his hand inside his shirt and felt for the bone amulet that hung from his neck. It was still and quiet to his touch. If there was any magic left inside the house, it was so small the amulet couldn't detect it. Hawk took his hand away from the amulet and looked round the drawing room. It was comfortably appointed, but nothing special. Cups and saucers had been carefully laid out on the table, along with milk and sugar and paper-lace doilies. Hawk looked hard at Tomb.

"What the hell is going on here, sir sorcerer?"

Tomb smiled slightly. "You'll find all kinds on the Street of Gods, Captain Hawk. Allow me to tell you the story of the Sundered Man. It's really very interesting. His life until his twenty-fourth year was quiet, comfortable, and quite uninteresting to anyone save himself. He was a junior clerk in the shipping offices. A little dull, but good prospects. And then the miracle happened. For reasons we still don't understand, he took it into his head to visit the Street of Gods. And whilst there he started to perform wonders and

speak prophecy. For twenty-four hours he walked the Street
of Gods, wrapped in Power and dispensing miracles. And
then . . . something happened. His followers called it the
final miracle. He levitated into the air, smiled at something
only he could see, and never moved again. He had somehow
become sundered from Time; frozen in a single moment
of eternity. Unmoving, unchanging, never aging. Nothing
could reach him, or harm him, or affect him in any way.

"It was never a very big religion, but those who'd been
with him on that day, and saw his wonders and heard him
preach, proved very loyal. They believed their man had
become more than human, a God who had stepped outside
of Time to commune with realities beyond our own. One
day, he would return and share his knowledge with the
faithful. That was twenty-two years ago. They waited all
that time, and then somebody killed their God."

"But why build a house like this on the Street of Gods?"
said Hawk. "Why not a church or temple, like everyone
else?"

"This was his house," said Sister Anna. "Or as near as
we could get to duplicating it. We built it around him,
room by room. We wanted him to feel at home when he
returned." She put her tray down on the table, picked up
the china teapot and silver tea-strainer, and poured tea for
all of them. She finally sat down facing them, and they all
sipped their tea in silence for a while. Hawk studied her over
his cup. There were deep lines in her face, and her eyes had
a bruised, puffy look, as though she'd been crying recently.
Her shoulders were slumped, and her gaze was polite but
unfocused. *Delayed shock*, thought Hawk. *The longer you
stave it off, the harder it finally hits*. He looked at Tomb
and raised an eyebrow, but the sorcerer seemed content to
leave the questioning to him. Hawk looked at Sister Anna
and cleared his throat.

"When did you first discover your God was dead?" he
asked carefully, trying not to sound too officious.

"Four o'clock in the morning, six days ago," said Sister
Anna. Her voice was calm and even. "One of our people

was always with him, so that he wouldn't be alone when he finally returned to us. Brother John was on duty. He went to sleep. He didn't know why. It wasn't like him. When he awoke, the God was no longer standing by the altar we made for him. He was lying crumpled on the floor, a knife in his heart. The blood was everywhere. Brother John spread the alarm, but there was no trace of the killer. We still don't know how he got in or out."

"Can we speak to this Brother John?" said Hawk.

"I'm afraid not. He took poison, later that day. He wasn't the only one. We all went a little crazy for a while."

"I understand."

"No you don't, Captain." Sister Anna looked at him squarely. "For twenty-two years we'd waited, devoting our lives to the Sundered Man, only to find it was all a lie. He wasn't a God after all. Gods don't bleed and die. He was just a man; a man with power perhaps, but nothing more. I'm the only one left now. The others are all gone. Some killed themselves. Some went home, to the families they'd given up for their God. Some went to look for a new God to worship. Some went mad. They all left, as the days passed and our God stayed dead."

For a while, nobody said anything.

"Is the body still there?" said Fisher finally.

"Oh, yes," said Sister Anna. "None of us wanted to move him. We didn't even want to touch him."

She led the way up the narrow stairs to the next floor and ushered them into a small, cosy bedroom. The Sundered Man was lying on the floor, curled around the knife that had killed him. There was dried blood all around the body, but no sign of any struggle. Hawk knelt down beside the dead man. There was only the one wound; no cuts to the hands or arms to suggest he'd tried to fend off his attacker. It was a standard-looking knife hilt; the kind you could buy anywhere in Haven. The dead man's face was calm and peaceful. Hawk got to his feet again, and shook his head slowly.

"There's nothing here to help us. Nothing I can see, anyway. Sister Anna, do you have any objections to our calling in the forensic sorcerers?"

"No," said Sister Anna. "Do as you wish, Captain. It really doesn't matter."

"Why did you stay?" said Fisher. "All the others left, but you stayed. What keeps you here?"

Sister Anna looked down at the body, and smiled slightly. "I was there, on the Street of Gods, twenty-two years ago, when it all began. I was just passing through, but he looked at me and smiled, and I stopped to hear him preach. He was magnificent. When he left I went with him, and from that moment on, I was always at his side. After he was taken from us, sundered from Time, I made this place my home, and waited for him to come back to me.

"How could I leave him? It didn't matter to me whether he was a God or a man. I stayed because I loved him, and always have."

The church of the Carmadine Stalker turned out to be a door in a wall. To one side of the door stood a pleasant little chapel of the Bright Lady, all flowers and vines and pastel colors. On the other side was an open, airy temple dedicated to the January Man. The door itself didn't look like much. It was six feet high and three feet wide, with peeling paint, splintering wood, and a large discolored steel padlock. It was the kind of door that in Hawk's experience usually fronted lock-up warehouses down by the docks, specialising in the kind of goods no one would publicly admit to wanting. He studied the door thoughtfully, aware that Tomb was watching him and waiting for him to comment. Obviously Tomb expected him to get all upset again. He was damned if he'd give the sorcerer the satisfaction.

"All right," he said equably, "It's a door. Do we knock or go straight in?"

"I'd better lead the way," said Tomb. "The Stalkers don't care for uninvited guests, with or without Council authority."

"Wait a minute," said Fisher. "If the Carmadine Stalker has been murdered, why are his followers still hanging around here?"

"They're waiting for him to rise from the dead. With all due respect, Captain Fisher, Captain Hawk, I think we should keep this visit as short and to the point as possible. The Carmadine Stalker was an unpleasant God of an extremely unpleasant Order. If his followers were to take exception to our presence, I'm not at all sure we'd get out of their lair alive."

"Don't worry," said Hawk. "We've been around. It takes a lot to upset us."

Tomb looked at him for a moment, and then turned to face the door. He gestured at the padlock, and it snapped open. He pushed the door, and it swung back, revealing a sickly green light. Tomb stepped forward into it. Hawk started to follow and then stopped short as the smell hit him. It was a thick, choking smell of corruption and decay. The green light seemed to take on a more sinister aspect, reminding Hawk of the corpse fires that danced on recently built cairns. He braced himself and followed Tomb into the light. Fisher followed close behind, her hand at her sword belt.

The door slammed shut behind them, and they found themselves in a long brick tunnel, slanting downwards, lit only by the eerie green light that came from everywhere and nowhere. The tunnel was only just tall enough for Fisher to stand upright, and no more than three or four feet wide. The brick walls were cracked and crumbling from age and neglect, and the floor was covered with pools of dark, scummy water. Mosses and fungi pockmarked the brickwork, and the smell of death and decay was almost overpowering. Far off in the distance a bell tolled endlessly, like the slow remorseless beating of a great brazen heart.

"What the hell is this place?" said Fisher, glaring warily down the tunnel.

"We're in the Stalkers' domain," said Tomb quietly. "A pocket dimension, attached to our reality but not actually a part of it. Follow me, please."

Tomb led the two Guards through an endless maze of narrow brick tunnels that twisted and turned and folded back upon themselves. The bell tolled on and on in the distance, but never seemed to draw any closer. Moisture dripped from the low ceiling and ran down the walls in sudden little streams. Hawk kept a wary eye on where they were going, but even so, the first priest caught him by surprise. The scrawny figure was sitting cross-legged in a niche set into the tunnel wall. He was old and shrivelled, corpse-pale and quite naked. Bones pushed out against his taut flesh. His breathing was slow and shallow, and his eyes were closed. A length of discolored steel chain ran from a heavy ring set in the wall to a great steel hook buried in the priest's shoulder. The tip of the hook poked out of the priest's flesh just below the armpit. From the way the puckered skin had healed around the sharp point, the hook had obviously been there a long time.

Tomb and the two Guards moved ahead quietly, trying to make as little noise as possible, but still the priest's eyelids crawled open as they passed. Hawk froze in his tracks, his hand at his axe. The priest had no eyes, only empty sockets, but still his head turned to face Hawk. He smiled slowly, revealing filed pointed teeth, and then his eyelids closed again. Hawk nodded to Fisher and Tomb, and they moved on. They passed more priests, from time to time, sitting unmoving in their niches in the walls. None of them stirred or spoke, but they all watched with empty eye sockets as the intruders passed.

And finally they came to a large, echoing chamber, empty save for a huge brass throne set in the centre of the open space. On the throne sprawled what was left of the Carmadine Stalker. Hawk moved slowly forward, keeping a watchful eye on the other tunnels leading off from the chamber. He stopped before the throne and wrinkled his nose at the remains of the Stalker. The discolored bones were held together by rotting scraps of muscle, and the grinning skull had been stripped almost clean of flesh. The Carmadine Stalker was an ugly sight in death, and

had probably looked even worse when it was alive. It had
to have been at least eight feet tall, with a broad chest and
a wide flat head. The arms and legs were too long, and
much thicker than a man's. There were vicious talons on
the hands and feet, and the grinning teeth were long and
pointed. Hawk tried to imagine what the thing must have
looked like in its prime, and for a moment his breath caught
in his throat.

"The Stalker was a grisly kind of God," said Tomb. His
voice was hushed, as though he was afraid of waking . . .
something. "Its religion was based around ritual sacrifice,
mutilation, and cannibalism. Let's keep this short, Captain
Hawk. This is a bad place to be. It's going to get even worse
when the Stalkers realise their God isn't going to rise from
the dead."

"All right," said Hawk. "Let's start at the beginning. How
was the Stalker killed?"

"Apparently it aged to death overnight, three days ago.
According to city records, the Stalker was at least seven
hundred years old. From the look of that body, I'd say a
lot of those years finally caught up with it."

"So the killer was a magic-user," said Fisher.

"Either that, or someone with an object of Power. Such
things aren't exactly rare on the Street of Gods."

Hawk took a quick look round the empty chamber, but
no obvious clues leapt to his gaze. "Is there anyone here
we can talk to, about how the killer got in and out?"

"No one here will talk to us, Captain. We're unbeliev-
ers."

"Then let's get the hell out of here. This place looks more
like a trap every minute."

Tomb nodded, and headed quickly for the tunnel mouth
that had brought them there. Fisher followed close behind,
sword in hand. Hawk backed out of the chamber, keeping a
careful watch on the dead God all the way. He had a strong
feeling that at any moment the tattered corpse might raise
its bony head and look at him . . . . He kept watching it until he reached a bend in the tunnel which cut off his view,

and then he turned and hurried after Tomb and Fisher. The great brass bell tolled on, its slow sonorous sound prophesying blood and doom.

Tomb led them confidently back through the maze of brick tunnels, and then stopped suddenly and bit his lip. Hawk frowned. By his reckoning, they were barely halfway back to the door on the Street of Gods. Tomb stood very still, his gaze vague and far away. Hawk looked quickly about him. The tunnel stretched off in both directions, silent and empty, bathed in the sickly light of the ubiquitous green glow.

"Something's coming," said Tomb softly.

Hawk drew his axe and Fisher hefted her sword. "What kind of something?" said Hawk.

"A group of men. A large group. Maybe as many as twenty. All of them armed. Apparently the Carmadine Stalker's followers don't want us to leave." Tomb shivered suddenly, and his gaze cleared. "I may be wrong, but I think it's very likely they're planning on sacrificing us to their God, in the hope it will help him return."

"All right," said Hawk. "You're the sorcerer. Do something."

"It's not that simple," said Tomb.

Fisher grimaced. "I had a feeling he was going to say that."

"There are things I can do," said the sorcerer, "but in this dimension they take time to prepare. You'll just have to hold them off for a while."

Hawk and Fisher looked at each other. "Hold them off," said Hawk.

"Twenty men," said Fisher.

"All religious fanatics, and armed to the teeth."

"Piece of cake."

The two Guards fell silent. In the darkness of one of the side tunnels, someone was moving. Whoever it was, was trying to be quiet, but even the faintest of sounds travelled clearly in the quiet of the tunnels. Hawk and Fisher stood side by side, weapons at the ready. Tomb gave the tunnel a quick glance, and then began muttering something under his breath. The first of the Stalkers came charging out of the side tunnel, and Hawk braced himself to meet him. The Stalker was tall and wiry, with a wide grin and staring eyes. He wore a dark, flapping robe, and carried a vicious-looking scimitar. He threw himself at Hawk, the curved blade reaching for the Guard's throat. Hawk batted the sword aside easily, and buried the axe in the Stalker's face on the backswing. The Stalker fell to his knees, blood coursing down his grinning face, and then he crumpled to the floor as Hawk jerked the axe free.

More Stalkers came boiling out of the side tunnel, their eyes glaring wildly. Swords and axes gleamed in the eerie green light. Hawk and Fisher launched themselves at their attackers. The flood of Stalkers stumbled to a sudden halt as Hawk and Fisher slammed into them. Hawk swung his axe in short, vicious arcs, and Stalkers fell dead and dying to the floor. Fisher stamped and thrust at his side, warding off the few Stalkers with reflexes fast enough to start their own attacks. Blood splashed the tunnel walls and collected in pools on the floor.

The narrow tunnel meant that only a few of the Stalkers could press their attack at one time, and Hawk and Fisher were more than a match for them. But even so, the fanatical hatred and fervour of the Stalkers drove them forward over the bodies of the slain, and step by step Hawk and Fisher were driven back down the tunnel. Tomb retreated behind them, still lost in his muttering.

Hawk swung his axe double-handed, trying to open up some space before him, but the press of bodies was too strong. Everywhere he looked there were darting swords and glaring eyes and pointed teeth bared in snarling smiles. Fisher gutted a Stalker with a quick economical cut, and turned to face the next attacker while the first was still falling. A sharp jolt of surprise went through her as the dying Stalker grabbed her legs with both arms and tried to bring her down. She met a flailing sword with an automatic parry, and tried to kick the Stalker away, but he hung on with grim determination. Blood from his wound soaked her trousers. The first twinges of panic had begun to gnaw at Fisher's self-control, when Hawk spotted her problem and cut through the Stalker's neck with his axe. The Stalker went limp and fell away, and Fisher kicked herself free. The whole thing had only taken a moment or two, but there was a cold sweat on Fisher's forehead as she hurled herself back into the fray.

I must be getting old, she thought sourly, *getting caught like that. Ten-to-one odds never used to bother me, either. Maybe I should get out of this business while I'm still ahead.*

She cut down one Stalker, gutted a second, and blinded a third. Blood flew on the air, and she grinned nastily.

Forget it; I'd be bored in a week.

The Stalker before her paused suddenly, his mouth gaping with surprise, and then his head exploded. Blood and brains spattered the tunnel roof and walls as Fisher jumped back, startled. There was a series of brisk popping sounds, and within the space of a few moments the tunnel floor was littered with headless bodies. Hawk and Fisher lowered their weapons, looked at each other, and then turned to stare at Tomb.

"Sorry it took so long," said the sorcerer calmly, "but that kind of spell is rather tricky to work out. You have to be very careful where you put the decimal point." He stopped suddenly, his head cocked to one side, listening to something only he could hear. "I think it might be wise to press on. There are more Stalkers on their way. Rather more than I can handle, I'm afraid."

"Then what the hell are we standing around here for?" snapped Hawk. "Move it!"

He pushed Tomb ahead of him, and the three of them ran swiftly through the brick tunnels, heading for the outside world. They hadn't gone far when they heard the sound of running feet behind them. Hawk and Fisher ran faster, urging Tomb on. He led them through the maze of tunnels with unwavering confidence, and suddenly they were through the doorway and out on the Street of Gods, blinking

dazedly in the bright summer sun. Tomb turned to face the
door, gestured sharply, and the door disappeared, leaving a
blank wall behind it.

"That should hold them," said Tomb. "Long enough for
us to make ourselves scarce, anyway. I trust you found the
visit useful?"

"Sure," said Hawk, his breathing slowly getting back to
normal. "Nothing like being chased by an army of murder-
ous fanatics to give you a good workout."

"Good," said Tomb. "Because I'm afraid I have to leave
you now. I do have other work to attend to, you know." He
produced a folded piece of paper from a hidden pocket, and
handed it to Hawk. "This is a list of Beings who may agree
to speak to you. It would help you to have an overview
of what's happening on the Street of Gods at the moment.
Beyond that, I'm afraid I really don't know what else to suggest. Tracking down murderers is a little outside my experience."

"We'll cope," said Fisher. "We're Captains of the Guard;
we don't need our hands held. Right, Hawk?"

"Right," said Hawk.

"I'm relieved to hear it," said Tomb. "If you need me
again, or any other member of the Squad, just ask around.
Someone will always know where we are. It's part of our
job to have a high profile. Good day."

He bowed politely to them both, and then set off down the
Street at a pace obviously calculated to prevent any further
discussion. Hawk looked at Fisher.

"He knows something. Something he doesn't want us
asking him about. I wonder what."

Fisher shrugged. "On the Street of Gods, that could cover
a whole lot of territory."

Charles Buchan sat on the edge of his chair, and waited
impatiently for them to bring Annette to him. The Sisters
of Joy were officially classed as a religion, and had one of
the largest establishments on the Street of Gods, but when
you got right down to it, their lounge looked like nothing

more than an upmarket brothel. Which wasn't really that far from the mark, if you thought about it.

The Sisters of Joy were an old established religion. Older than Haven itself, some said. It had branches all across the Low Kingdoms, to the impotent fury of equally old and established, but more conservative, religions. The Sisters had started out as temple prostitutes for a now forgotten fertility Goddess, probably not unlike the Bright Lady, and had somehow evolved through their discovery of tantric magic into something far more powerful. Not to mention sinister.

Tantric magic is based on sex, or to be more exact, sexuality. Basically, the Sisters of Joy drained people's strength and vitality through sex, leeching at their very life force. The stolen energy gave them greatly extended life spans, and made them powerful magicians, but only as long as the energy level was maintained. They needed a lot of people to maintain their power and their long lives, but human nature being what it was, the Sisters were never short of visitors. Or victims, depending on how you looked at it.

Tantric magic wasn't strictly speaking part of the High Magic at all, having its roots squarely in the older, less reputable Wild Magic, which was partly why most modern sorcerers would have nothing to do with it. The other reason was that women were a hell of a lot better at tantric magic than men, and the High Magic was still largely a male province. So the High Magic was socially acceptable, while tantric magic very definitely was not. The Sisters of Joy didn't give a damn. They went their own way, as they always had. Their door were always open, day and night, to those who came to them in need or despair. The Sisters offered care and comfort and affection, and in return bound all who came to them in a tightening web of emotional dependency and obligation. There were those who said the Sisters of Joy were addictive, and that those who fell under their influence became little more than slaves. No one said it too loudly, or too publicly, of course. It wouldn't have been wise.

Buchan got up out of his chair, and began to pace up and

down. They would bring Annette to him soon.

The lounge was almost indecently luxurious. A thick pile carpet covered the floor, and the walls had disappeared behind a profusion of paintings and hanging tapestries, most of them obscene. Perfumes sweetened the air. There were comfortable chairs and settees and love seats, and delicately crafted tables bearing wines and spirits and cordials, and every kind of drug or potion. Nothing was forbidden here, and it was all free. To begin with. The Sisters of Joy had amassed a considerable fortune over the many centuries, and they still received very generous donations from their grateful clients. No one ever mentioned blackmail, of course. It wouldn't have been wise.

With an effort, Buchan stopped himself pacing. It was a sign of weakness, and he couldn't afford to be weak. He looked again at the brass-bound clock on the mantelpiece, and frowned. He couldn't stay long, or Tomb and Rowan might wonder where he was. They might ask questions. So might Hawk and Fisher. He would have to be careful around the two Guards. They had a reputation for sniffing out secrets and getting to the bottom of things. Buchan was always careful to go disguised when he made his visits to the Sisters of Joy, but no disguise was perfect, especially on the Street of Gods. Still, only the Quality knew for sure of his connection with the Sisters, and they didn't know as much as they thought they did. And when you got right down to it, the chances of the city aristocracy deigning to discuss such matters with the likes of Hawk and Fisher were pretty damned remote.

The Quality wouldn't discuss one of their own with outsiders. Even if they had disowned him.

He smiled slightly. It wasn't that long ago he'd been an important figure in the Quality, a member in good standing and much in demand. No one cared about his reputation then; it just gave them something juicy to gossip about. The Quality do so love their gossip. But even the most sybaritic, most debauched member of the Quality had drawn the line at his associating with the Sisters of Joy. The Sisters were

beyond the pale, utterly forbidden. First his friends talked
to him about it, and then his enemies. His Family forbade
him to visit the Sisters, on pain of disowning him. But he
couldn't stay away, and he wouldn't tell them why, so in the
end the Quality had turned their back on him, and his Family
had cut him off without a penny.

He didn't care. Not really. He had a new life in the God
Squad, and he had his Annette.

And then the door opened, and she came in. His breath
caught in his throat as it always did, and he stood there for
a long moment, just drinking in the sight of her. She was
tall and slender and graceful and very lovely. Long blond
hair curled down around her shoulders, and her eyes were
the same blue as his own. She smiled at him, the special
smile she saved for him and him alone, and ran forward
into his waiting arms.

Tomb slowly climbed the stairs to Rowan's room, a silver
tray floating on the air beside him, bearing a cup of steaming
tea. The sorcerer was worried about Rowan. She'd been ill
on and off for months now, and she still wouldn't let anyone
call in a doctor to see her. She didn't believe in doctors,
preferring to dose herself with her own foul mixtures.
Tomb didn't know what went into them, but every time
Rowan prepared a fresh batch in the kitchen, the cook
threatened to quit. Having smelt the fumes himself on more
than one occasion, Tomb didn't blame her. If the smell had
been any stronger, you could have used it to pebble-dash
walls. Tomb's mouth twitched, but he was too worried to
smile. Rowan had been taking her vile doses for weeks,
and she was still no better. If her condition didn't improve
soon, he'd bring in a doctor, no matter what she said. He
couldn't stand to see her looking so drawn and tired.

He moved quietly along the landing and stopped outside
Rowan's door. He knocked politely, and glared at the tea
tray when it showed signs of wavering. There was no reply,
and he knocked again. He looked round vaguely as he
waited. Rowan rarely answered the first few knocks. She

liked her privacy, and often she didn't care for company. Rowan had never been what you'd call sociable. Tomb sighed quietly, and shifted his weight from one foot to the other.

The house seemed very quiet. Buchan was out, and it was the servants' day off. Tomb had been a member of the God Squad for almost eleven years now, and he knew the house and its moods well. Of late, however, the quiet seemed to have an almost sinister nature; a quiet of unspoken words and too many secrets. Of course, the house was used to secrets. No one came to the God Squad with an entirely clean past. Which was probably why so few of them stayed long. It wasn't everyone who could cope with the eccentric realities of the Street of Gods. Tomb had seen many warriors and mystics come and go down the years. He hoped Rowan would stay. She was special. He knocked on the door again, a little louder.

"Rowan? It's me, Tomb. I thought you might like a nice cup of tea. Can I come in?"

There was still no reply. Tomb opened the door and entered quietly, the tea tray floating uncertainly behind him. Rowan was fast asleep, looking small and helpless and worrisomely frail in the oversized bed. Tomb pushed the door shut, and the tea tray flew forward and settled on the table beside the bed. Rowan stirred slowly without waking, and then settled again. She'd disarrayed the bedclothes in her sleep, like a fretful child, and Tomb moved quietly forward to straighten them. He stood back, looked round the room, and then looked at Rowan again. She seemed to be sleeping peacefully now. There didn't seem to be anything else he could do. There was no reason for him to stay.

He sat down on the chair beside the bed. The room was the same featureless square as his own, but she'd done more to personalize hers in the short time she'd been there than he had in all his eleven years. There were oil paintings on the walls that she'd executed herself. They showed promise. A cuddly toy with a stitched-on smile lay on the floor beside the bed. Rowan liked to take it to bed with her when the others were away on cases and she was left alone in the house at night. Tomb could understand that. There are times we all need something to cling to in the night. The rug on the floor was a new addition. Tomb had spent a whole afternoon in the markets with her, trying to find one just the right shade to complement the bedclothes.

She stirred again in her sleep, and Tomb looked at her quickly, but she didn't waken. Tomb sat and watched her for a while. He liked to watch her. He could quite happily have sat where he was all day and all night, watching over her, caring for her. Loving her. He smiled slightly. He never used the word love except in his thoughts. He'd told her once how he felt about her, after an hour or so of talking around the subject while he worked up his nerve, and the best he could say of the outcome was that at least she hadn't laughed at him. She just told him that she didn't care for him, and seemed to think that was the end of it. Tomb smiled tiredly. If only it was that easy. He hadn't asked to fall in love with her. She wasn't especially bright or pretty. But she owned his heart and always would, and there wasn't a damn thing he could do about it.

Reluctantly he got to his feet. Rowan could wake up anytime now, and he'd better not be here when she did. He didn't want to upset her. He left the room quietly, and eased the door shut behind him. He made his way back down the stairs, frowning slightly as he tried to work out what he ought to do next. There was a hell of a lot of paperwork that needed seeing to, but then there always was. It could wait a little longer. He supposed he could take a walk down the Street, talk to people, get a feel of how the Street was reacting to Hawk and Fisher's arrival.

Or he could go to see Le Bel Inconnu.

He stopped at the bottom of the stairs. He couldn't go now. It was far too dangerous, with Hawk and Fisher out on the Street. They wouldn't understand. But he couldn't stay away either. It was already too long since his last visit. He glanced back up the stairs. Rowan would be all right.

The protective wards around the house would make sure she wasn't disturbed. And if she wanted anything, she only had to call and Tomb would hear her, wherever he was. She knew that.

He hurried down the hall, took his cloak from the rack, and swung it round his shoulders. He pulled the hood forward, adjusting it so that its shadow covered his face. He could have used a disguise spell, but there were too many places on the Street where magic couldn't be relied on.

And this was too important to take unnecessary risks.

The sorcerer Tomb opened the door with a wave of his hand, and went out onto the Street of Gods.

Hawk and Fisher slogged up and down the Street of Gods, working their way through the list of names Tomb had given them. Hours passed, but the sun overhead didn't move. It was noon on the Street of Gods, and had been for several days. Robed acolytes hurried past them on unknown missions, heads bowed to show respect and humility, and to avoid having to see churches and temples more splendid than their own. The street preachers were still working themselves into hysterical rages and setting fire to each other, but no one was paying much attention except the tourists. Hawk and Fisher tramped grimly back and forth, getting what information they could from the Beings that Tomb had named as potentially helpful, and doing their best to ignore the wonders and terrors that thronged the Street.

The Night People were an old necromantic sect, not as well-supported as they had once been. Their High Priest met Hawk and Fisher in the Ossuary, the Cathedral of Bone. Intricate patterns of polished bones formed the floor and walls and ceilings of the Ossuary. Some were recognisably human. Others were so large and grotesque that Hawk preferred not to think about where they might have come from originally. The air smelt of musk and cinnamon, and strange lights flickered in far off windows. All the time they were there, Hawk had a strong feeling they were being watched, as though something awful and implacable lurked just out of sight, waiting patiently for him to drop his guard. He kept his hand near his axe.

The Night People were blind, their eyelids stitched together, but they all moved and spoke with an eerie certainty that bordered on the unnerving. Hawk did his best to ignore the uneasy prickling on the back of his neck, and asked to see the nameless Being the Night People worshipped. The High Priest shook his head slowly. Only the faithful might see God, and that sight was so glorious it burned out the eyes of all who saw. Hawk tried to press the matter further, but the High Priest would not be moved. He wouldn't even ask questions on the Guards' behalf. Neither would he allow them to question the faithful. No one knew anything that might help the Guards. No one knew anything about the God killings. No one knew anything about anything.

Hawk and Fisher went from church to temple to meetinghouse, and the message was always the same. The Hanged Man was polite but unhelpful. Sweet Corruption wasn't even polite. The Lord of the New Flesh refused even to see them.

And so it went the length of the Street, until finally they came to the Legion of the Primevil. The Legion's church was a tall building of spires and domes and crenellated towers. There were magnificent stained-glass windows, and flags and banners in a dozen different hues. Some other time Hawk might have been impressed, but as it was, all he could think of was his aching feet. It had been a long day.

The Legion priests, however, were frankly disturbing. Each and every one had a staring alien eye embedded somewhere in his flesh. It was large and crimson with a dark split pupil, and it blazed unblinkingly from forehead, chest, or hand. In a few cases it had displaced one of the priest's original eyes, and it bulged uncomfortably in the too-small socket, glaring balefully at the world. Legend had it that the Legion was the means whereby an ancient Being from another plane of existence was able to observe the world of men.

The High Priest seemed happy enough to talk to Hawk and

Fisher, but could do little to help them. With three Beings murdered in a matter of weeks, gossip ran wild on the Street of Gods. But no one knew anything for sure. People were scared. So were some of the Beings. Everyone was looking for a villain; someone to blame and strike back at. No one had mentioned God War yet, but everyone was thinking about it.

Hawk and Fisher talked with the High Priest for some time, trying to avoid staring at the great crimson eye that glared unblinkingly from his forehead. Nothing much came of it until right at the end, when the High Priest suddenly leaned forward on his throne and fixed Hawk with his unnerving stare.

"Tell me, Captain. Have you ever heard of the Hellfire Club?"

"No," said Hawk cautiously. "Can't say that I have." He looked at Fisher, and she shook her head slightly.

The High Priest leaned back on his throne, his expression unreadable beneath the glowing third eye. "Ask Charles Buchan, Captain. He knows."

And that was all he would say. In a matter of minutes the two Guards were back on the Street again, not much wiser than when they'd started. It was still midday, and the air was uncomfortably warm. Hawk and Fisher decided simultaneously that what they really needed to help put things in perspective was a stiff drink. Or two. Accordingly, they made their way to the nearest temple dedicated to John Barleycorn, and ordered a ceremonial libation in tall glasses. They took their drinks and settled into a private booth at the back of the temple where the lights were comfortably dim. Hawk stretched out his legs with a luxurious sigh, and propped his aching feet on a nearby chair. Fisher took off one of her boots and massaged her toes. Some moments were just too precious to interrupt, but eventually they turned their attention to their drinks, and the matter at hand.

"All right," said Hawk. "Let's run through what we've got. Three Beings are dead. Since they are dead, I think it's safe to call them Beings rather than Gods. The Dread Lord died nine days ago. His body had been torn apart. The Sundered Man was stabbed to death six days ago. And the Carmadine Stalker apparently aged to death three days ago. Doesn't take a genius to spot the pattern, does it?"

"A murder every three days," said Fisher. "With another due sometime today, if the pattern continues."

"Right," said Hawk. "And there's nothing we can do to prevent it. We don't have enough information, and no one will talk to us."

Fisher smiled briefly. "Why should the Street of Gods be any different from the rest of Haven?"

Hawk sniffed. "Anywhere else, I could persuade someone to talk to us. But the mystic was right; strong-arm tactics aren't going to work here. If I start shoving my axe in a Being's face, I'll probably end up snapping at flies on a lily pad. Intimidation is very definitely out. That just leaves diplomacy."

"I'll leave it to you," said Fisher. "I don't have the knack."

"I had noticed," said Hawk. "What do we have on the killer? He comes and goes at will, even when the temples are heavily guarded by well-armed fanatics. Which means he's either invisible, which means a sorcerer, or a master of disguise. Or it's someone they expect to see, someone they don't recognise as a threat.

"Each Being died in a different way, and as far as we can tell, none of them had anything in common. So how does the killer choose his victims? At random? Dammit, I don't even know where to start on this case, Isobel."

"Don't give up so easily. Look at it this way. The killer has to be immensely strong, and able to pass unseen. So how about a supernatural killer, like a vampire? He could get past the guards by shapeshifting into a bat or a mist, and he'd be more than strong enough to tear apart the Dread Lord. It would even explain why all the killings took place in the early hours of the morning."

Hawk thought about it. "It's a possibility, lass, but I

can't believe the Beings wouldn't have protective wards specifically designed to keep out supernatural vermin like that. Everybody else does, that can afford them. No, Isobel; I think magic is the key here."

"You mean a rogue sorcerer?"

"Maybe. An invisibility spell would get him past the wards and the guards, and then he could use magic to blast apart the Dread Lord and age the Stalker to death."

"But then why use a knife on the Sundered Man?"

"To be misleading?"

"That makes my head hurt," said Fisher. She took a long drink from her glass, and frowned hard as she concentrated. "Wait a minute, though. . . . Turn it around. You can also see the killings as being linked by a lack of magic. The wards couldn't keep the killer out. The magic keeping the Stalker alive failed. So did the magic keeping the Sundered Man out of time. And maybe it was only magic that was holding the Dread Lord together. He was hollow, remember? So maybe what we're looking for is a sorcerer, or a man with an object of Power, that can dispel magic and leave the Beings vulnerable."

"An object of Power that dispels magic," said Hawk slowly. "The Exorcist Stone?"

"Oh, hell!" said Fisher. "One of the God Squad as a God killer? Come on, Hawk."

"They're the only ones that can use the Exorcist Stone."

"But the Council put a compulsion on them to prevent them from misusing it!"

Hawk smiled sourly. "If this was an easy case, they wouldn't need us to solve it. It has to be one of the God Squad, Isobel; it's the only theory that fits all the facts. The killer must have found some way to bypass the geas."

"We don't dare accuse any of them without a hell of a lot of proof," said Fisher. "These people have friends in high places. Sometimes literally. Dammit, Hawk, we're supposed to be working with these people. How can we keep something like this from them?"

"Very carefully," said Hawk. "Whichever one of them is the killer has already destroyed three Beings. I don't think they'd hesitate to kill a couple of Guards who were getting too close to the truth."

They sat in silence for a while. "So what are we going to do?" said Fisher.

"Take things one step at a time," said Hawk. "To start with, I think we'll have a word with Charles Buchan, and see what he knows about the Hellfire Club. Whatever that is."

"He was the only one of the God Squad to be named during our investigation," said Fisher thoughtfully.

"Yes," said Hawk. "Interesting, that. But perhaps just a little too obvious. Unless we're supposed to think that . . . "

Fisher groaned and shook her head, and reached for her glass again.

Hawk and Fisher left the temple of John Barleycorn, and found that night had fallen without warning. Here and there, street lamps pushed back the night as best they could, but darkness pooled thickly between them. Unfamiliar stars shone in the night sky, forming alien constellations that bore no resemblance to those seen elsewhere in Haven. There was no moon, and the night air had a feverish, unsettled quality. The Street of Gods was almost deserted. The street preachers had disappeared, and only a few hooded figures still bustled back and forth on their eternal errands. Hawk frowned unhappily. The Street wouldn't normally be this quiet just because it suddenly got dark. But with a God killer on the loose, most people had clearly decided against taking unnecessary risks.

The two Guards headed back down the Street toward the God Squad's headquarters. For once, Hawk's internal clock agreed with the Street's time, and he was quietly looking forward to a good supper. He wondered what kind of cook the Squad had. He usually did the cooking at home. Fisher hadn't the temperament for it.

They'd just passed the mouth of a narrow alleyway when they heard a muffled cry for help. As one, they spun quickly to face the dark opening, weapons in hand, but didn't immediately rush in to see what was happening. In the Northside, a cry for help in a dark place was bait for a trap as often as not. A single lamppost glowed dully at the end of the alley, casting more shadows than light. There was no sign of whoever had called out. Hawk looked at Fisher, and she shrugged briefly. It might just be genuine. Hawk nodded, and stepped cautiously into the alleyway. Fisher moved quietly at his side, the amber lamplight gleaming on her sword blade.

Hawk scowled unhappily as the two of them moved slowly down the alley, alert for any sign of movement. The buildings on each side were dark and silent, with no lights showing at their windows. A low scraping sound cut across the quiet somewhere up ahead, and the two Guards froze where they were, eyes straining at the shadows. Nothing moved. The silence was so deep it was like a physical presence. Fisher gently tapped Hawk's arm to get his attention, and nodded at the structure just ahead and to their right. A window shutter was open just a crack. No light shone from inside. Fisher padded silently forward, and set her back against the wall next to the shutter. She reached up with her sword and eased the shutter open. She waited a moment, and when there was no reaction, she moved away from the wall and peered in through the window. She couldn't see anything but the darkness, and there wasn't a sound anywhere. Fisher looked back at Hawk, and shrugged.

She turned to move away, and the window burst outwards as a dark figure smashed through it. Powerful arms grabbed Fisher from behind and hauled her back through the shattered window. Hawk lunged forward, but she'd already disappeared into the dark building. He took a deep breath, and pulled himself up and through the window in one quick, graceless movement.

He hit the floor rolling and threw himself to one side. He scrambled up into a defensive crouch, axe held out before him, and then froze where he was. He couldn't see a damn thing, and all he could hear was his own carefully controlled breathing. There was always the chance the attacker had already fled, but Hawk didn't think so. This whole thing smelled like a planned ambush. He started to wonder why and then pushed the thought firmly to one side. That didn't matter now. All that mattered was what had happened to Fisher.

He bit his lip angrily. He couldn't just stay put. The attacker's eyes were bound to be more used to the dark than his. For all Hawk knew, the bastard was already creeping up on him from behind. That thought was enough to push Hawk into a decision. Moving quickly but carefully, he put his axe down on the floor, ready to hand, and then eased a box of matches from his pocket. He opened the box and took out a single match. He pressed it against the side of the box and then hesitated. It had to light on the first try. If it didn't, the sound would be enough to give away his position and what he was doing. He'd be an easy target. Hawk took a deep breath, let it out, and struck the match.

Light flared at his hand, illuminating the room. Fisher was down on one knee, on the other side of the room. A dark, hooded figure stood over her, knife in hand. Hawk dropped the match and snatched up his axe.

"Isobel! Hit the floor!"

Fisher threw herself forward without hesitation, and in that brief moment before the match reached the floor and went out, Hawk aimed and threw his axe with all his strength behind it. Darkness filled the room. There was the sound of a body hitting the floor, and then silence. Hawk scrabbled at his box of matches and quickly lit another match. Light flared up again. The hooded figure was lying on its back, the heavy steel blade of the axe buried in its chest. Fisher was in a defensive crouch not far away, unharmed, sword at the ready. Hawk let out a long sigh of relief. He took his emergency stub of candle from his pocket and lit it with the match. He put it down on the floor and walked over to Fisher.

"You all right, lass?"

"A few cuts and scratches, that's all. My cloak protected me from anything worse."

Hawk nodded, relieved, and leant over the body to retrieve his axe. He grabbed the hilt, and the body came alive.

It surged up off the floor, reaching for Hawk's throat.

He stumbled backwards, trying to pull the axe free, but the blade was tightly wedged in the figure's breastbone. Heavy, powerful hands closed around Hawk's throat.

Fisher loomed up behind the attacker, snarling with rage, and her sword flashed once in the candlelight as it swept round to sink deep into his neck. Hawk pulled at the hands round his throat and felt them loosen. Fisher jerked her sword free in a flurry of blood and struck again, grunting with the effort. Blood flew again as the sword half-severed the head from the body. Hawk pulled free, and with that, all the strength seemed to go out of the hooded figure, and it fell to the floor and lay still. Hawk kicked the body several times, just to be sure, and then tugged his axe free. Fisher knelt down and pulled back the figure's hood. Her hand came away bloody, but that wasn't what made her gasp. Even in the dim light, both she and Hawk recognised the face.

It was the Dark Man. The sorcerer Bode's double.

"Damn me," said Hawk shakily. "How many times do we have to kill him before he stays dead?"

"It's not the same man . . . " said Fisher slowly. "The build's different. Not nearly as muscular. Which suggests that Bode didn't stop with just the one double. . . . "

"So there could be any number of them still out there," said Hawk. "Just waiting for another chance at us."

"Great," said Fisher. "Just what this case needs. More complications."

4

Hellfire and Damnation

"The Hellfire Club?" said Charles Buchan. "Of course I've heard of it. But I don't see what it's got to do with anything."

"Let us worry about that," said Hawk. "You just tell us what you know."

The God Squad and the two Guards were back in their headquarters' drawing room, catching up on what they'd all been doing. Tomb in particular seemed very interested in Hawk and Fisher's reactions to the various Beings they'd seen, and kept pressing them for details. Rowan looked utterly disinterested, and kept rubbing at her forehead as though bothered by a persistent headache. She'd spent most of the day in bed, sleeping. It didn't seem to have helped her much. Buchan looked calm and completely self-possessed, as always. Hawk's stomach rumbled. The sooner they got this over with and settled down to a good supper, the better.

"The Hellfire Club is the latest craze among the younger Quality," said Buchan easily. "They get dressed up in strange costumes, take whatever drugs are fashionable, chant rituals, and try to raise something from the Gulfs so they can sell their souls to it, in return for power and miracles. It's harmless."

"It doesn't sound harmless," said Fisher. "What if they succeed?"

"They won't," said Buchan. "It takes more than a few chants and bad intentions to raise a demon. No, Captain, it's just playacting, nothing more. A way to let off some steam and upset their parents at the same time. If it even looked like they were succeeding at raising something nasty, they'd either run a mile or faint from shock."

"Either way, it's still illegal," said Hawk flatly. "Any kind of religious rite or ceremony is expressly forbidden outside the Street of Gods. It's the only way to keep these things under control. Why haven't you reported the Hellfire Club to the Council?"

"We did," said Rowan, her voice too tired to hold its usual acid. "We reported it to the Council, they reported it to the Guard, and your superiors filed the report carefully away and ignored it. The Hellfire Club is run by the Quality for the Quality, and the Guard knows better than to try and interfere. The Quality don't give a damn about the law. They don't have to. They own it."

"Not always," said Fisher. She looked at Hawk. "I think we'd better do something about this, Hawk."

Hawk frowned. "It's not really our province, Isobel. Our authority is limited to the Street of Gods, for the time being."

"Come on, Hawk," said Fisher. "Doesn't it seem just a little too coincidental to you that soon after the Quality start their rituals, the Beings start dying? There must be a connection, or why would the priest have told us about the Club?"

Hawk looked at Buchan. "She's got a point."

"They won't talk to you," said Buchan. "The Quality don't talk to outsiders about anything."

"They'll talk to us," said Hawk. "Isobel and I talk very loudly, and we don't take kindly to being ignored."

Buchan sighed. "In that case, I'd better come with you. I talk the Quality's language. Maybe I can keep them from killing you. Or vice versa."

The Quality were throwing a party.

Nothing unusual in that. The city aristocracy based their

lives around parties, politics, and the pursuit of pleasure. Not necessarily in that order. But this one looked to be something rather special, and Hawk and Fisher were determined to be there. According to Buchan, at this particular party the Hellfire Club would be in session.

They made their way through High Tory, that part of Haven exclusively reserved for the Quality. While Hawk and Fisher looked interestedly around them at the magnificent halls and mansions, Charles Buchan kept up a running commentary on the Quality, and how they fitted into Haven life. Hawk and Fisher knew most of it already, but let him talk. There was always the chance they'd learn something new; about Buchan, if not the Quality.

There were exactly one hundred Families in the Quality, never more, and together they formed a separate little state within the city-state of Haven. The only way in was to be born a part of it, or marry into it. Personal wealth wasn't enough. A man could be poor as a church mouse, and still look down on the wealthiest of merchants, if he had the right blood in his veins. The aristocracy's wealth was mostly inherited, though some of it still came from rents and the like; between them the Quality owned most of Haven and the surrounding lands. They could have been even richer if some of that wealth had been invested in Haven's businesses, but that just wasn't done. Trade was for the lower, merchant classes. Technically, the Quality were subordinate to the elected city Council, which represented King and Parliament, but in reality both sides were careful not to put pressure on the relationship from either direction.

Hawk let Buchan drone on, listening with one ear at most. He had his own problems. The party they were going to gate-crash was being hosted by Lord Louis Hightower, and that might lead to complications. The present Lord Hightower had come to his estate after the tragic deaths of both his father and elder brother. Both men had died violently during the course of enquiries into murders on which Hawk had been the investigating officer. No one

blamed him for the deaths. Officially, he'd been cleared
of any negligence. It remained to be seen what Lord Louis
Hightower felt about the matter. The Quality had its own
private ideas on justice and retribution. Officially, the Guard
were exempt from the Code Duello, or any other form of
vengeance, but that was just officially. In this, as in so
many other matters, the Quality went its own way when
it suited them.

The cold winter air was brisk and bracing after the art-
ificial summer warmth of the Street of Gods. Hawk kicked
moodily at the dirty slush that covered the road and the
pavement. The Council was supposed to scatter grit and
salt on the road at the first sign of approaching winter, but
they always left it too late, with the excuse of not wanting
to waste money by acting too soon. So this year, as every
year, a gritting that could have been done in an hour or two
would now take two or three days, during which business
would grind to a halt all over the city. Typical.

Hightower Hall loomed up ahead, dominating the surroundings at the end of Royal Row. It was a long, impressive
two-storey building of the best local stone, the great wide
windows blazing with light. A high stone wall surrounded
the luxurious grounds, topped with iron spikes and broken
glass. Four men-at-arms in chain mail manned the tall
iron gates. They looked very professional. Hawk slowed
his pace, and put a hand on Buchan's arm to stop his
monologue.

"Looks like they're expecting trouble," he said quietly,
nodding at the men-at-arms. "The Quality's security meas-
ures aren't usually so ostentatious. And you can bet that if
there are four armed men in clear sight, there are a hell of
a lot more patrolling the grounds and scattered throughout
the Hall. Are you sure this is the right place, Buchan? I'd
hate to fight my way in and then find I was at the wrong
address."

Fisher sniggered. "Wouldn't be the first time."

"This is the place," said Buchan. "I still have a few
contacts with High Society. The Hellfire Club meets here

tonight. And Captain, please: no violence. The God Squad has its reputation to think of. Besides, we shouldn't have any trouble getting in; I've acquired invitations for all of us."

"Pity," said Fisher. "I was quite looking forward to a good dust-up. There's nothing like kicking a few supercilious backsides to put you in a good mood."

Buchan looked at her sharply. She didn't appear to be joking. "Please, Captain Fisher. Promise me you won't kill anyone."

"Don't worry about it," said Hawk. "We'll be on our best behavior. We'll just ask our questions, get some answers, and leave. Right, Isobel?"

Fisher sniffed. "You're getting old, Hawk."

"I'm not even sure what we're doing here," said Buchan. "The Hellfire Club may be technically illegal, but there isn't a Court in Haven that would convict a member of the Quality on such a minor charge."

"You're probably right," said Hawk. "Personally, I don't give much of a damn about the Hellfire Club itself; but there's got to be a reason why that priest pointed us in their direction. It may just be professional jealousy, but I don't think so. Somewhere, there's a connection between the Club and the God murders, and I want to know what it is."

The men-at-arms at the gate looked suspiciously at Buchan's engraved invitations, and passed them back and forth amongst themselves before reluctantly opening the gates and standing back. Buchan retrieved the invitations while Hawk and Fisher strolled casually into the grounds as though they owned the place. Buchan smiled politely at the men-at-arms and then hurried after Hawk and Fisher as they strode off up the gravel pathway that led to Hightower Hall.

"Not the front door," he said quickly. "The men-at-arms might have been fooled by the invitations, but no one else will be. Anyone with real authority will take one look at your Guards' cloaks and slam the door in our faces. Only the Quality and their personal servants are allowed into a Quality home. Our only chance of crashing this party is to sneak in through the servants' entrance at the back. Once inside, everyone will just assume you're wearing costumes in rather bad taste."

Hawk and Fisher looked at each other, and Buchan's heart sank as he took in their expressions. "We don't sneak in through the back door," said Hawk firmly. "We're Captains in the city Guard. We go in through the front door. Always. Right, Isobel?"

"Right, Hawk." Fisher smiled slowly. "And anyone who tries to slam the door in my face will regret it."

The two Guards headed determinedly for the front door, their hands resting on the weapons at their sides. Buchan wished briefly but vehemently that he was somewhere else, anywhere else, and followed them.

Hawk pulled the bell rope and knocked firmly on the front door. Fisher kicked it a few times for good measure. After a discreet pause, the massive oak door swung open, revealing a tall and very dignified butler dressed, as tradition demanded, in slightly out-of-date formal wear. He had a thick mane of carefully groomed grey hair, and a pair of impressively bushy eyebrows that descended slowly into an even more impressive scowl as he took in the two Guards standing before him.

"Yes?" he said, disdainfully, his mouth tucking in at the corners as though he'd just bitten into an especially sour lemon.

"We're here for the party," said Hawk easily. "Show him the invites, Buchan."

Buchan quickly held them forward. The butler didn't even bother to look at them. "There must be some mistake . . . sir. This gathering is exclusively for the young gentlemen and ladies of the Quality. You have no business here . . . sir."

"My partner and I are Captains in the city Guard," said Hawk. "We're here on official business."

The butler gestured sharply, and two men-at-arms appeared behind him, swords in hand. The butler smiled slightly, his eyes cold and contemptuous.

"You forget your place, Captain. Your petty rules and regulations have no bearing here, among your betters; your lords and masters. Now kindly remove yourselves from these premises. At once."

"You're not going to be reasonable about this, are you?" said Hawk.

"Leave now," said the butler. "Or I'll have my men set the dogs on you."

Hawk hit him briskly, well below the belt, waited a moment as the butler folded forward, and then punched him out. By the time the two men-at-arms had reacted, Hawk had drawn his axe and Fisher had drawn her sword, and the two Guards had walked over the butler's unconscious body and into the hallway. The men-at-arms looked at them, and then at Charles Buchan, the most famous duellist in Haven, and quickly sheathed their swords.

"I'm not getting paid enough for this," said one flatly, and the other nodded. "The party's that way."

Hawk and Fisher smiled politely, and strolled unhurriedly in the direction the man-at-arms had indicated. Buchan stepped over the butler and went after them.

"You promised me you'd behave," he said urgently.

"We haven't killed anyone yet," said Fisher.

Buchan had a horrible suspicion she wasn't joking.

A footman in a rather garish frock coat appeared from nowhere, and apparently assuming they were official guests, led them to the main ballroom. Servants, laden with trays of food and wine, swarmed back and forth through the wide corridors. Hawk gradually became aware of a growing clamour up ahead, the sound of hundreds of voices raised in talk and laughter and argument. It grew steadily louder as the footman led them to a pair of huge double doors, and then the sound burst over them like a wave as the footman pushed open the doors. Hawk and Fisher and Buchan stood together in the doorway a moment, taking in the sight and sound of the Quality at their play.

Hundreds of bright young things were packed into the huge ballroom, dressed in their finest. There were all sorts of fashions and costumes, ranging from the ridiculous to the grotesque. Hawk wasn't surprised. The younger aristocracy always had a taste for the garish. The whole point of elite fashion was to choose clothes that no one but they would be seen dead in. And yet the crowd wasn't composed of only young people. There were a significant number of older men and women, suggesting that the attractions of the Hellfire Club spread across a larger proportion of the Quality than Hawk had expected. His scowl deepened as he took in some of the more sinister costumes: jaggedly cut leathers and bizarrely dyed furs, metal-studded bracelets and spiked chokers. One striking woman dressed in black rags and tatters carried a live snake wrapped around her bare shoulders.

A band of musicians was playing loudly in the gallery, but no one was dancing. That wasn't what they'd come for. Hawk tore his gaze away from the Quality and looked around the great ballroom. He'd known smaller parade grounds, and the ceiling was uncomfortably high overhead, much of it lost in shadow. Three huge chandeliers of polished brass and cut glass lit the scene below with hundreds of candles. Hawk looked at them uneasily. They had to weigh half a ton each, and the thick ropes used for lifting and positioning them looked almost fragile by comparison. Hawk decided he'd keep an eye on them. He didn't trust chandeliers. They always looked unsafe to him.

He noticed that the footman was still with them, waiting to be dismissed. Hawk nodded briskly, at which the footman bowed and left. Buchan watched this thoughtfully. Hawk and Fisher had surprised him with how comfortable they were with servants. As a rule, it was a knack most people didn't have unless they were born into it. Most people found servants intimidating. Hawk and Fisher didn't. Of course, there was a simple explanation; Hawk and Fisher weren't impressed by servants because they weren't impressed by anything.

Buchan looked out over the ballroom. It was a long time since he'd been welcome here. Almost despite himself, his

mind drifted back to his last visit to Hightower Hall. Lord
Roderik Hightower had been away on one of his werewolf
hunts, and Louis was still in the army then. But Lady
Hightower was there, to speak on behalf of the Family.
The Hightowers and the Buchans had been friends for
generations, but that hadn't prevented the Lady Hightower
from informing him in cool, passionless tones that unless
he agreed to end his relationship with the Sisters of Joy, he
should consider himself banned from High Society from that
moment on. Buchan had said nothing. There was nothing
he could say.

You're a fool, Lady Hightower had said. *You have good
friends, position and wealth, a promising future in politics,
and all the advantages your Family have given you. And
you've thrown it all away for the sake of those women. You
disgust me. Get out.*

He had stood there and taken it all in silence, and when
she was finished he nodded once, politely, and left. He'd
stayed away from High Tory ever since. Now he was back,
among familiar sights and sounds once again. He hadn't
realised how much he'd missed it all. He emerged from his
reverie, suddenly aware that Hawk was speaking to him.

"We'd better split up," said Hawk. "We can cover more
ground that way, and hopefully we'll be less conspicuous
on our own."

"Suits me," said Fisher. "What exactly are we looking
for?"

"Beats me," said Hawk. "Some connection between the
Hellfire Club and the God murders. It could be anything.
A person, a place, a belief . . . anything."

Fisher frowned thoughtfully. "These people, Buchan . . . they worship the Darkness, right?"

"Essentially, yes," said Buchan.

"They try to make deals with it. Offer it things, in return
for power."

"Yes, Captain."

"Would they go as far as sacrificing people to the Dark?"
Buchan hesitated. "I don't know. Some might, if they

thought they could get away with it."

"And it's only a step from killing people to killing Beings," said Hawk. "If they have already made a deal with the Darkness, and it's given them enough power to kill Beings . . . "

"Then we could be in a lot of trouble here," said Fisher.

"Nothing changes," said Hawk. "All right, let's make a start. Each of you choose a direction, and start walking. Be discreet, but don't be afraid to ask pointed questions. I'm not leaving here without some answers. Oh, and Isobel; let's try and avoid Lord Hightower. Right?"

She nodded, and Hawk slipped into the milling crowd, letting the ebb and flow of people take him where it would. Everywhere he looked there were flushed faces and over-bright eyes and strained, brittle laughter. The sense of anticipation was almost overwhelming. And yet without Hawk's foreknowledge of what the Hellfire Club was about, it would have been easy to see this as just another party. Most of the Quality here were young, half of them barely out of their teens. Partying desperately, squeezing what joy they could out of their lives before the inevitable time when they would have to take on their duties as part of the Families. There were only a few options open to the Quality: For the men it was either politics or the army, for women it was marriage and children. Perhaps that was why they'd formed the Hellfire Club, in search of pleasure and power with no price to pay. Or at least, no price they believed in.

Hawk knew better. No one encounters the Darkness and comes away unscathed. The scars on his face throbbed briefly with remembered pain.

He moved deeper into the crowd. Hundreds of people filled the huge ballroom from wall to wall, but Hawk wasn't impressed. He'd seen grander gatherings in his time. And the more he looked, the more he became aware of the nervous undercurrent in the party's mood. The laughter was too sudden and too loud, and the general brittle good cheer wasn't fooling anyone but themselves. Many of the

Quality were drinking like fish, but no one seemed to be
drunk. Hawk frowned slightly. It was as though the Quality
were trying to nerve themselves up to something. Something
frightening . . . and dangerous.

Buchan wandered aimlessly through the crowd, looking
for familiar faces. Most of them here were too young to
remember him, and his shame, but clearly there were some
who did. They looked the other way, or turned their backs
on him. None of them wanted to talk to him. It wouldn't
be safe. Some of his shame might rub off on them. Buchan
grabbed a glass of wine from a passing servant's tray and
drank deeply. Not a bad vintage. A damn sight better than
the cheap muck he usually drank.

He hadn't been aware of how lonely he'd been until he
came back here, and realised how much he'd had to give
up. All the food and wine and comforts. The security of
belonging. Hawk and Fisher might be contemptuous of High
Society, but they couldn't know what it meant, to be a part
of it. The Quality were Family and friends and lovers, and
more than that. They shared your life from the cradle on.
On good days and bad days and empty days, they were
always there. They seduced and protected you, loved you
and hated you, and kept you safe from the outside world;
made you feel part of a greater whole. It was comforting
and reassuring to have the same faces always around you,
people who understood you sometimes better than you knew
yourself. He hadn't realised how much he missed it all, and
how much there was to miss.

The God Squad was his family now, but they were no
substitute for what he'd given up. Tomb was a friendly
enough sort, but he had no interest in anything save his
magics and his books, and he was too sober by far. The
sorcerer meant well, but the God Squad was his life, and
nothing else really mattered to him. And Rowan was a pain
in the posterior. Spent all her time poring over ancient
books and papers, and filling the house with chemical stinks.
He'd tried to talk to her about her theories and beliefs, but
most of the time she just answered his questions with

grunts and monosyllables. On the few occasions when she condescended to explain something to him, he was damned if he could follow it, for all his expensive education. All he could grasp was that Rowan didn't believe in anything much but desperately wanted to believe in something. So desperately that there was no room in her life for anything but the search.

Buchan looked slowly around him. It was a long time since he'd considered how much he'd given up for his darling Annette. And though he loved her more than anything else in his life, there were times he hated her too, for what that love had cost him. He pushed the thought firmly aside, and moved on through the crowd of turned backs and averted faces.

Hawk finally spotted a familiar face, and strolled nonchalantly over to join him. Lord Arthur Sinclair was well on his way to being drunk, as usual. The last time Hawk had seen Lord Sinclair, he and Fisher had been clearing up after the Haven elections. Sinclair had stood as a candidate, on the No Tax On Alcohol Party. Also known as the Who's For A Party Party. He never even looked like winning, but he didn't let a little thing like that dissuade him to holding a celebration party long before the results came in. It was two days before he sobered up long enough to ask who'd won.

Sinclair was a short, round little man in his mid-thirties, with thinning yellow hair and uncertain blue eyes. He smiled a lot, at nothing in particular, and was rarely without a glass of something in his hand. He was a third son, who'd never expected or been intended to inherit the Family estates. He had no talents, no gifts, no aptitudes, and no interest in anything but parties. His friends thought him a pleasant, harmless little chap. Always ready for a song or a joke or another drink. His Family treated him like dirt for the most part, and tried to pretend he didn't exist. He had no sense of self-esteem, and no chance to build any. And then his father and both his brothers died in the same battle, and the title and estates fell to him, along with the not inconsiderable Family fortune. His mother died soon after, from a broken heart some said, and he was left all alone. He'd been Lord Sinclair for almost five years, and had spent most of that time trying to drink himself to death, for want of anything better to do.

Hawk approached Sinclair and nodded familiarly to him. Sinclair smiled back. He was used to being treated as a friend by people he didn't recognise or remember. There's no one so popular as a drunk with money.

"Good party," said Hawk.

"Marvelous," said Sinclair. "Dear Louis never stints on these affairs. Would you like a drink?"

Hawk nodded, and Sinclair poured him a generous glass of pink champagne from one of the bottles in a nearby ice bucket. Hawk sipped at it cautiously, and refrained from pulling a face. Far too sweet for his taste, but that was the Quality for you. With their taste for sugar in everything, it was a wonder they had any teeth left at all.

"So, when does the excitement start?" said Hawk, trying not to sound too vague.

"Soon," said Sinclair. "Do I know you?"

"We've met briefly, in the past."

Sinclair smiled sadly. "That covers rather a lot of ground, I'm afraid." He emptied his glass, and filled it again. "You're new here, aren't you?"

"That's right," said Hawk. "I'm here about the Club. The Hellfire Club."

"Aren't we all. My little fancy seems to have caught on. I had no idea it would prove so popular."

"This was your idea, originally?"

"Indeed. My one and only good idea. Would you like to hear about it? I do so love to talk about it, and everyone else has heard the story by now. You know about me, of course. Everyone does. My parents' generation never tire of holding me up as a Bad Example. Not that I care. I never wanted to be head of the Family. I was happy with my parties and my poetry. I used to write poetry, you know. Some of it was quite passable. But I don't do that anymore. I couldn't see the point. When they all died and left me alone, I couldn't see the point in anything anymore. I mean, they weren't always very nice to me, but they were my Family, and one or other of them was always there, making sure I didn't hurt myself too badly. I do miss them.

"I don't believe in anything much anymore, but I keep looking. There has to be something; something *real* to believe in, apart from just chance. Only sometimes, I think there isn't. I think that rather a lot, actually, but a few drinks usually helps. I tried religion for a while. I really thought I was on to something there. But there were so many religions, and I couldn't choose between them. They couldn't all be right, but they all seemed so sure of themselves. I've never been sure of anything. Then I met this fellow on the Street of Gods. Marvelous young sorcerer chappie; Bode, his name was. He gave me the idea for the Hellfire Club. He was very interested in the power you could get from tapping the darkness within you. Of course, the idea seems to have got a bit muddled since all these other people got involved in the Club. . . .

"I liked Bode. He was always good company. Bit too intelligent for his own good, but then, that's sorcerers for you. Had this very intense girlfriend, all sarcasm and deep insights. I was ever so upset when I heard he died just recently."

He drained his glass, and looked thoughtfully at another bottle in the ice bucket. Hawk's thoughts were racing furiously. He'd come here looking for a connection between the Hellfire Club and the God murders, but he seemed to have stumbled across a connection to a completely different case. Sinclair must have met Bode while the sorcerer was carrying out his mysterious commission on the Street of Gods. But who was this girlfriend Sinclair met? Hawk frowned as another thought came to him. Given the appearance of the second Dark Man on the Street of Gods, maybe the two cases weren't separate after all. Maybe everything was connected. . . .

Hawk had just decided he'd better press Sinclair for more details, when someone tapped him hard on the shoulder from behind. He turned round to find himself facing three large and openly menacing members of the Quality. They were all taller than he, and they all looked as though they worked out regularly with heavy weights.

"Can you smell something?" asked the leader of the group loudly. He sniffed at the air and grinned nastily. "I smell a Guard. No mistaking that stench. But what's a dirty little Guard doing at a private party? A private Quality party?"

"I'm here on official business," said Hawk, careful to keep his voice calm and unthreatening. It was obvious the three Quality were looking for trouble. Anywhere else he might have obliged them, but not here. The ballroom was full of hundreds of their friends, all of them Quality. They could cripple him or kill him, and nothing would be done. And he daren't lift a finger to defend himself. You could, under very rare circumstances, arrest a member of the Quality, even put them on trial, but it still had to be kid gloves all the way. The Quality were under no such restrictions. At best, they'd give him a good kicking and put him in hospital, just for the fun of it. He didn't want to think what they might do to Fisher.

"An official investigation," said the group's spokesman. "Did you hear that? Doesn't it just make you shiver in your boots? I don't give a damn about your investigation, Captain. No one here does. We don't have to. This is our place. We don't allow your sort in here. Is that clear?"

Hawk started to reply, and the leader hit him open-handed across the face. Hawk saw the blow coming and rode most of it, but he took a step backwards despite himself. His cheek flared red from the impact, and a thin trickle of blood ran down his chin from a split lip.

"You're going to have to talk louder, Captain. I can't hear you if you whisper."

Hawk smiled suddenly, and a fresh rill of blood ran down from his split lip. The leader of the three Quality hesitated, suddenly uncertain. The Guard's smile was cold and unpleasant, and far too confident for his liking. He glanced quickly about him to check his two friends were

still there. His confidence quickly returned. The Guard
wouldn't dare try anything. The first sign of violence,
everyone would turn on him. He opened his mouth to
say so, and the Guard's hand shot forward and fastened
onto his trouser belt. The Guard took a good hold, and
then twisted it suddenly and jerked upwards. The leader's
voice disappeared as his throat clamped shut. Tears sprang
to his eyes as his trouser crotch rammed up into his groin. He
tried to stand on tiptoe to ease the pain, but it was all he could
do to get his breath. He grabbed desperately at the Guard's
arm, but the thick cords of muscle didn't give an inch. The
Guard twisted again, crushing his groin, and a fresh wave
of pain welled up through his belly, sickening him.

Hawk brought his scarred face in very close to the Quality
leader's. "You don't talk like that to a Guard. Not now, not
ever. Is that clear?"

The leader nodded, and tried to force out an answer.
Hawk twisted his hold viciously, and the man's face went
white.

"Is that clear?"

The leader nodded frantically, and Hawk let him go. He
collapsed into the supporting arms of his friends, who looked
just as scared and confused as he did. Hawk fixed each of
them in turn with his single cold eye.

"Take your friend and get out of here," he said calmly.
"I don't want to see your faces again. Is that clear?"

They nodded quickly, and half led, half carried their
friend away. Hawk watched them go. The trick to situations
like that was to take out the leader as quickly and as painfully
as possible. It's not a question of what you do, as what you
make them think you're prepared to do. Take control of the
situation away from them. Make them sweat. Make them
afraid. You learn things like that in Haven. He looked
casually around him, but the incident had passed so quickly
that no one seemed to have noticed anything. He turned back
to Sinclair, who was studying him thoughtfully.

"You know, that really was very impressive," said Sinclair. "I wish I could do things like that."

"You could learn," said Hawk.

"No, I don't think so. It probably involves a lot of things like practice and discipline and hard work. Not really me, I'm afraid. Did you know you have blood on your chin?"

Hawk took out his handkerchief and wiped carefully at his mouth and chin. "You have to be able to stand up for yourself. It helps keep the flies off."

Sinclair smiled. "Like I said, not really me. It's not important. You see, I don't matter. Not to anyone. Never have and never will." He stopped, and looked at Hawk. "Is something wrong, Captain?"

"No. You just reminded me of someone I used to know. Someone who felt like that."

"What happened to him?"

Hawk looked across at Fisher, on the other side of the room. "He found someone who believed in him."

Fisher had found herself to be very popular. Young men gathered around her, plying her with drinks and sweets and smiles, and vying with each other for her attention. The young rakes and blades were always on the lookout for a new pretty face, the more exotic the better. And compared to the carefully groomed and painted flowers of the Quality, the six-foot muscular blonde in the Guard's cloak seemed very exotic indeed. The female members of the Quality seemed caught between ostentatiously ignoring her and glaring at her when her back was turned.

Fisher didn't care much for the Quality, singly or en masse. More money than they knew what to do with, and nothing to give their lives meaning except an endless round of love affairs, duels, and Family vendettas. The ones with any guts went into the army; these here at the party were the ones who'd stayed behind. Which was why they joined the Hellfire Club. Their lives were so empty that there was nothing left but to play at being bad in the hopes of shocking each other, or at least their parents.

Fisher pumped the young men unobtrusively with leading questions, but didn't get much in the way of answers. The Quality were too busy making fools of themselves trying to impress her. They began to get on her nerves after a while, and when hints that she'd prefer to be left alone fell on deaf ears, she started to wonder if punching out one or two of them might help to get her message across. She'd just selected her first target, when a loud confident voice cut across the young men's babble, and quickly sent them all packing.

Fisher looked her rescuer over carefully. He was a little taller than she, elegantly slender, and dressed in well-cut, sombre clothes. He was in his late twenties at most, and good-looking in a dark, traditional way, though there was a self-satisfied look to his eyes and mouth that Fisher didn't like.

"Lord Graham Brunel, at your service," he said smoothly. "I do hope those boys weren't bothering you too much. I'm afraid the Club has grown so popular now that we seem to be letting just anyone in. I'll have to speak to Louis about it. Now, may I know your name, dear lady?"

"Isobel," said Fisher carefully. "This is my first time here."

"Yes, I thought it must be," said Brunel. "I'm sure I'd have remembered so distinctive a beauty as yourself if we'd met before. That is a Guard's cloak you're wearing, isn't it? Is it the real thing, by any chance?"

"Oh, yes," said Fisher. "It's real."

"You really must tell me how you came by it. I'm sure it's a fascinating story."

"You wouldn't believe how fascinating," said Fisher. "Have you been with the Hellfire Club long?"

"Almost from the beginning, my dear. Arthur Sinclair came up with the idea originally, bless his booze-rotted brain, but it was Louis Hightower and I who brought the Club together and made it what it is."

"But have you achieved any results?" said Fisher.

"You'd be surprised," said Brunel. "We're getting close to something very powerful, Isobel. I can feel it. Something so awful and magnificent it'll tear this dreary little city apart. But there's nothing to be worried about, my dear, I promise you. You just stay close to me, and I'll keep you safe."

"That's very kind of you," said Fisher, "But I already have an escort."

"Drop him. You're with me now."

Fisher smiled at him. "Fancy yourself, don't you?"

Brunel looked at her uncertainly. "I beg your pardon?"

"You haven't achieved anything, have you, Brunel? In all the time you've been running this Club, have you raised a single demon, contacted a Power, or even managed to make the lights flicker a little?" She paused a moment while Brunel went red in the face and struggled for words. "I thought not. The Hellfire Club, when you get right down to it, is just another game. Another excuse to get dressed up, drink too much, and have a good time jumping at shadows. Just a bunch of overgrown kids. I don't think I'll be staying."

Brunel reached out quickly and took her by the arm. "Oh, but I really must insist, my dear. You've been asking a lot of questions, but you haven't told us anything about yourself. I think it's time you told me who you really are."

Fisher slowly raised her arm despite his hold, and showed him the silver torc at her wrist. "Isobel Fisher, Captain of the city Guard. Now get your hand off me or I'll break your fingers."

Brunel's face was suddenly harsh and ugly, all charm fled. His fingers dug into her arm muscle, trying to hurt her. "A spy. A dirty stinking Council spy. You're not going anywhere, Captain. We can use you, in the Hellfire Club. Some of us have been wondering if a human sacrifice might not be just what we need, to make the breakthrough we've been looking for. We were going to use one of the servants, someone who wouldn't be missed, but you'll do nicely. No one's going to miss you; no one even knows you're here, right?"

Fisher smiled at him. "I think this has gone far enough." She reached out with her free hand and clapped him on the shoulder. Her thumb found the exposed nerve behind the collarbone, and pressed down hard. Brunel's face screwed up as the pain hit him, and his hold on her arm loosened. She shrugged free of him, and pulled his face close to hers. Brunel tried to pull away, but the stabbing pain paralysed him.

"No human sacrifice, Brunel. Not tonight or any other night. The Guard's going to keep a close watch on you from now on. And if we even suspect you're thinking about a human sacrifice, we'll come back here in force and drag each and every one of you out of here in chains. We've left you alone because you're harmless. Stay that way, or I guarantee you'll spend the rest of your days walking the treadmill under the city gaol. Got it?"

She let him go and he staggered back a pace, clutching at his shoulder. He tried to scowl at her, but couldn't meet her eyes. He turned and disappeared into the crowd, and was swallowed up in a moment. *This is a waste of time,* thought Fisher. *We're not going to find our God killer here.* She looked around her for Hawk and Buchan.

Buchan wandered through a crowd of averted faces, feeling not unlike the ghost at the feast. Word of his arrival had circulated quickly through the gathering. Backs turned at his approach, and murmurs rose and fell as he passed. The Quality, young or old, liked to think of itself as being above petty moralities and restrictions, but when you got right down to it, their affairs and debaucheries still followed very strict guidelines. For all the freedom that wealth and position brings, there remained things that were simply not done. And when it came to matters of Family and inheritance, the Quality were very conservative. Wives and children were important; they continued and preserved the precious bloodlines, without which there would be no hundred Families, no Quality. So for an only son, the last of his line, to turn his back on marriage and make regular visits to the Sisters of Joy was simply unacceptable.

There was a stir in the crowd to his left, and Buchan looked round in mild surprise to find someone approaching him. His first thought was that he was about to be asked to leave, but as the crowd fell away he saw that it was the party's host, Lord Louis Hightower. Buchan winced mentally though his face remained impassive.

The Lord Hightower was of average height and stockily built, much like his late father. As a second son, he had been spending a quiet and not unsuccessful life in the army when his father and mother died in the same night, victims of a werewolf's curse. His elder brother had been murdered some months previously. So he resigned his commission and came home, and now he was the Lord Hightower, one of the leading lights in the Quality and chief organizer of the Hellfire Club. He and Buchan were the same age, and had been friends, once. Buchan waited for Hightower to come to him, and then bowed politely. He was ready for almost anything except the sad, exasperated sigh with which Hightower greeted him.

"What the devil are you doing here, Charles? I wouldn't have thought this Hellfire nonsense was in your line."

"It isn't," said Buchan. "But it may have a connection with a case I'm working on for the Squad. And what do you mean by calling it nonsense? I thought you were one of the people running the Club."

Hightower shrugged. "It's amusing. And interesting, sometimes. But I don't get carried away with it, like some people I could mention. I might have known it would take something like this to bring you back here." Hightower looked at him steadily. "It's been a long time, Charles. Too long."

Buchan smiled. "Not everyone would agree with you, Louis. I don't go where I'm not welcome. I have that much pride left."

"You're always welcome in my home, Charles. You know that."

"Yes. But my presence in your house would do you no good at all. People would talk."

"Let them. You think I care more about my reputation than my friends?"

"You have a position to maintain now," said Buchan firmly. "You're not just a second son any longer. You're *the* Hightower, the head of the Family. You have responsibilities to them now, as well as yourself. And to whatever poor woman you eventually decide to marry. You shouldn't even be talking to me, really."

"As head of the Family, I do have some authority. People may mutter, but they won't say anything. Not in public. It's good to see you again, Charles. I saw your mother last week. She's looking well. Are they still not talking to you?"

"As far as I know. I haven't been back there in a while, either. As far as they're concerned, I don't exist. And perhaps that's for the best."

"Are you still . . . ?"

"Visiting the Sisters? Yes."

"They'll destroy you, Charles. They destroy all their victims, in the end." Hightower took in Buchan's face, and raised a hand defensively. "All right, I know. You don't want to talk about it. And I can't ask you about the case you're working on, because you never talk about that, either. Is there anything you do feel free to discuss?"

"I was sorry to hear about your parents, Louis. It must have been a shock."

"Yes, it was. The funny thing is, I'd been expecting my father's death for some time. He'd been looking old and tired ever since Paul was murdered. You never knew my brother, did you? He was a good sort, and always too brave for his own good. Father thought the world of him. He took Paul's death hard.

"He hated being retired, too. Didn't know what to do with himself after he left the army. Dabbled in politics for a while, but . . . I was out of town when he and mother died, on manoeuvres. I miss them, you know. Every day there's something that makes me think *I'd better ask Dad about that*, or *I wonder what Mother would say* . . . and then I remember, and the day seems a little colder. I miss them, Charles. I really miss them."

"You ought to get married," said Buchan firmly. "It's not sensible, you and the servants rattling around in this huge old place by yourself. Get yourself a wife and fill the place with children. Do you a world of good."

Hightower laughed. "Just like the rest of my Family. Can't wait to see me safely married and settled down. I always said I'd only marry for love, Charles; never just for duty. You can understand that, can't you?"

"Yes," said Buchan. "I understand."

They stood together a moment, wanting to say more, but not sure how. They'd pretty much exhausted the few things they still had in common, and what remained of their lives now was separated by a gulf neither of them could cross.

"So," said Hightower finally. "Is there anything you can tell me about the God Squad business that brings you here?"

"You've heard about the God murders, I take it? Well, my associates turned up a lead that suggested there may be a connection between the Hellfire Club and the killings."

"I don't see how," said Hightower. "It's all a lark, nothing more. Just another excuse for a party. The rituals are fun, but no one seriously expects anything to come of them. Well, most of us don't, anyway. There are always a few idiots. But most of the Club are only here to annoy their Families. A sign of rebellion, without having to risk anything that matters."

"What got you involved?" said Buchan. "I wouldn't have thought this was your kind of thing."

"It isn't. But there are a great many young ladies who are interested, so . . . "

Buchan laughed. "I might have known. Is it true most of your rituals take place in the nude?"

"Quite a few of them, yes." Hightower grinned. "And that's not all we do in the rituals that our Families wouldn't approve of."

They laughed together, and then the double doors burst open and a sudden silence fell across the room as everyone turned to look.

The Dark Man stood in the doorway. Blood splashed his shapeless furs and dripped thickly from both ends of the long wooden staff in his hands. He was grinning broadly, and his eyes were fixed and wild. He looked slowly round

the crowded ballroom, and the Quality fell back before his
unwavering gaze. Death and violence hung around him
like a shroud. In the silence that greeted his arrival they
could hear voices moaning and crying out in pain from
the corridor outside. Hawk and Fisher pushed their way
through the crowd toward him, blades at the ready.

A man-at-arms appeared behind the Dark Man. Bruised
and bleeding heavily, he nevertheless flung himself at the
Dark Man and tried to get a choke hold on him. They
staggered back and forth for a moment, and then the Dark
Man twisted suddenly and threw the man-at-arms over his
shoulder. He hit the floor hard and lay still, groaning quietly.
The Dark Man raised his staff and brought it sweeping down
with vicious force, striking his victim again and again and
again. Blood flew and bones shattered. The limp body
jumped and jerked under the rain of blows, even after the
man was clearly dead.

There were stifled screams and moans of horror from the
Quality, and a few of the braver men moved forward. Hawk
yelled for them to stay back. The Dark Man slowly raised
his head and grinned at those advancing on him. There was
blood on his face, none of it his. The handful of men slowed
to a halt and looked at each other uncertainly.

"Dammit, stay where you are!" yelled Hawk, his voice
cutting across the rising babble. "He's too dangerous! I'm
city Guard. My partner and I will take care of him."

The Quality moved quickly to get out of the Guards' way.
The Dark Man grinned bloodily and threw himself at those
still between him and his intended victims. He struck out
furiously with his staff, not caring who he hit, and men and
women alike fell to the polished floor with broken heads
and stove-in ribs. The Quality began screaming again, and
fought each other in their panic to get out of the Dark Man's
way as he headed toward Hawk and Fisher. A handful of
men threw themselves at the killer, but he shrugged them
off easily, not even feeling their fists. One of them grabbed
at the Dark Man's leg from the floor. Without looking
down, the Dark Man kicked the man free, and then stamped

viciously on his chest. The man lay still, and the Dark Man
moved on. The rest of the Quality hung back. It would have
been different if they'd had weapons, but wearing weapons
in a friend's house wasn't done. So they'd all left their
swords at the door.

And then finally Hawk and Fisher reached the Dark Man,
and his grin widened. He threw himself forward, swinging
his staff in a powerful horizontal arc. Fisher ducked under
it and ran the Dark Man through, her sword blade grating
between his ribs. His grin never wavered, and he struck at
her arm with his staff. Fisher's hand went numb and she had
to jump back, leaving her sword wedged in the Dark Man's
ribs. Blood ran thickly down his sides, but he took no notice
of it, his eyes following Fisher as she backed away.

Hawk stepped in and swung his axe from the killer's blind
side. The Dark Man spun round at the last moment and
parried the blow with his staff. The impact almost wrenched
the axe from Hawk's hand. The two men circled each other
warily, searching for an opening. Hawk felt a sudden chill
rush through him, as he realised the Dark Man was a better
fighter now than he had been the first few times they'd met.
It was as though he was learning with each new fight, each
new death . . . as though each new Dark Man was the same
man. . . .

What the hell am I fighting here?

He misjudged a blow with his axe, and the end of the
staff clipped him just above the ear in passing. The world
rocked around him for an instant, and the Dark Man pressed
forward. Hawk backed away quickly, holding onto his axe
more by instinct than anything else. The Dark Man swung
his staff, and Hawk ducked at the last moment. He stumbled,
off balance, and looked up just in time to see the staff coming
round on the backswing for a blow that would crack his skull
like an eggshell. There wasn't even time to close his eye.

And then Fisher darted in from behind, and cut at both
the Dark Man's legs with her knife, hamstringing him. He
fell forward onto his hands and knees as his legs gave out,
the muscles half severed. He didn't make a sound, even

when Fisher took hold of her sword and jerked it out of his ribs. Instead, he slowly got his feet under him, one at a time, and stood up, still clinging to his staff. Fisher backed away. Hawk gaped at him blankly. It just wasn't possible with wounds like that . . . the leg muscles had to be tearing themselves apart. The pain must be hideous. . . .

The Dark Man moved toward Fisher, one step at a time. Blood coursed down his legs. He was still grinning. Hawk looked about for inspiration. His gaze fell upon a heavy rope tied to a wall bracket. He followed the rope upward, and realised it was supporting one of the huge chandeliers. It took him only a moment to see that the Dark Man was standing almost directly underneath the chandelier. Just a few more steps . . .

"Isobel!" he called urgently. "Hold your ground! Let him come to you!"

Fisher shot him a quick glance and then took up a defensive stance where she was, favouring her bruised arm as best she could. *There had better be a bloody good reason for this, Hawk, because I don't think I can stop him on my own. He's not human.*

The Dark Man shuffled slowly forward, leaving a trail of blood behind him. The Quality were hushed and silent, watching with widened eyes. It was one thing to join the Hellfire Club for a few easy thrills, but quite another to come face to face with blood and death and suffering at such close quarters. The Dark Man shuffled forward, his grin widening. Fisher braced herself, and Hawk cut the rope with his axe.

The Dark Man just had time to see a shadow gathering around him and look up, and then half a ton of polished brass and cut glass hammered him to the floor. The sound of the crash echoed on and on. He lay still, and for a long moment no one said anything. And then the Dark Man slowly got his hands underneath him and tried to lever himself up. The chandelier lifted an inch or two, and then settled itself more firmly. Blood burst from the Dark Man's mouth, and he fell forward and lay still again. Hawk stepped in, raised his axe, and struck down with all his strength. There were a few shocked cries from the Quality as blood spurted and the Dark Man's head rolled free, but Hawk paid them no heed. He wasn't taking any chances.

Buchan made his way through the crowd to join Hawk and Fisher. "That was some fight. You might have let it last long enough for me to join in. Do either of you know who he was? What he was doing here?"

"Tracking us, I think," said Hawk. "It's to do with a murder case we worked on before we joined the God Squad."

"I see," said Buchan. "Do you want to explain that to these people, or shall I?"

"I think it might be better if none of us did," said Fisher. "Hawk, let's get the hell out of here. The regular Guard will be here soon; let them handle it."

Hawk looked around him. "All these people hurt, because of us . . . "

"We don't know that," said Fisher. "Now let's go."

Hawk nodded, and let Buchan lead him and Fisher out of the ballroom. Behind them, the Quality had closed in around the Dark Man's body and were kicking it viciously. Hawk looked back once, and then looked away. Buchan smiled grimly.

"If nothing else, Hawk, you've got to admit the Quality know how to throw a party. You never know what's going to happen next."

5

Secrets Come to Light

Rowan sat up stiffly in bed and groaned loudly. She hurt all over, and her mouth tasted foul. She felt more tired now than when she'd gone to bed. She reached painfully over to the bedside table and grabbed the cupful of potion she'd prepared earlier. She took a quick sip, then leaned back against the headboard and looked unhappily at the sickly green stuff in the cup. Putting mint in to flavour it had definitely been a mistake. It must have clashed with something. On the other hand, it couldn't taste much worse than her mouth did anyway. She lifted the cup determinedly while her nerve held out, and gulped the horrid stuff down. It tasted even worse than she felt, and she indulged herself by pulling awful faces as she put the cup down on the table. She paused in mid-grimace as she noticed the steaming cup of tea on the silver tray, also resting on the bedside table. Her mouth flattened into a thin line. Tomb had been in her room again. She was going to have to do something about Tomb.

Rowan began to feel a little better as the potion began its work, and she pushed back the bedclothes and swung her legs over the side of the bed. She picked up the cup of tea, looked at it for a moment, and then sipped at it cautiously. It was strong and sweet, and a pleasant warmth moved through her. Say what you would about Tomb, and she could think of a lot, most of it based around the word *irritating*, the fact remained that he made a good cup of tea. Still, she was definitely going to have to do something about him. She'd made it as clear as she could that she had no feelings of any kind for him and would be just as happy if he'd find somebody else to pester, but he seemed determined not to get the point. Maybe she should try something more direct, like hitting him. She didn't really want to be unpleasant about it, but it might be kinder in the long run. It certainly wasn't fair to let him go on hanging around like this.

She smiled sourly as she sipped her tea. Not that she had time for any more complications in her life, but if someone had to fall for her, why couldn't it have been Buchan? All right, he was a few years older than she, but he still had one hell of a body. He was more experienced than Tomb, more sophisticated; he would have understood the situation. They could have had a marvelous, uncomplicated affair that was fun while it lasted but nothing to fret over when it was finished. But no. The dashing, debonair, handsome Charles Buchan couldn't be bothered to look at a dumpy little thing like her. He had to save himself for those stinking bitches at the Sisters of Joy. She sighed wistfully. Such a waste of a good man . . . but then, that was the way the world went. Nothing was what it seemed, nobody could be trusted, and there was no point in believing in anything unless you could hold it in your hand and check it for flaws. A harsh philosophy, but better than nothing.

She looked at the travelling clock on the mantelpiece. Buchan should be back from the Hellfire Club soon, along with the two Guards. She scowled, thinking about Hawk and Fisher. They were going to be trouble; she'd known that from the moment she first met them. They didn't understand what was happening on the Street of Gods, but that wouldn't stop them from charging blindly in, trying to put things right by brute force. They were fools, but they were dangerous fools. She yawned suddenly, and took a long, slow stretch. She looked wistfully at her warm, comfortable bed. Just another half-hour's rest would feel so good. . . .

She heard footsteps coming up the stairs, and tensed. Her head was still too muzzy for her to See who it was. The footsteps came unhurriedly along the landing and stopped outside her door. There was a long pause, followed by a hesitant knock. Rowan relaxed, and let out her breath in a quiet sigh. She knew that knock.

"Come in, Tomb."

The sorcerer opened the door and came in, shot a quick glance at Rowan to see how she was, and then smiled winningly at her. "Just thought I'd look in and check you were up. The others will be back soon."

"Yes, I know. I'm feeling much better, thank you."

"That's good. I'm glad."

"Tomb?"

"Yes, Rowan?"

"Do you think you could shut the door? It's rather drafty in here."

"Oh. Yes. Of course."

He pushed the door shut, turned back, and tried his winning smile again. Rowan realised she was still holding the teacup and put it down on the tray.

"Thank you for leaving me tea again. That was very sweet of you."

"You're welcome." The sorcerer grinned and nodded his head, pleased.

Just like a puppy that's done a trick correctly, and wants to be patted and told he's a good dog, thought Rowan tiredly. *How the hell can a first-class sorcerer like Tomb be such an idiot when it comes to women? I really don't need this. Not now.*

Tomb's smile slowly disappeared, and he shuffled his feet uncertainly. "You know, Rowan, I really am getting rather concerned about you."

"You are? Why?"

"Well, this isn't the first time you've been ill like this, is it?"

"There's no need for you to worry. I'll be fine. I know what I'm doing."

Tomb visibly braced himself to disagree with her. "I know you have a lot of faith in your potions, Rowan, but I really would be a lot happier if you'd let me call in a doctor, just to look you over and make sure it's nothing serious."

Rowan glared at him. "I do not need a doctor. How many times do I have to tell you, Tomb? My health and how I look after myself are none of your business."

"But I do worry about you."

"Don't. There's no reason why you should be so concerned. Just because I'm part of the God Squad doesn't give you the right to hover around me like a broody hen. You're an acquaintance of mine, Tomb; nothing more. Is that clear?"

Tomb nodded slowly. "Yes, Rowan. Very clear."

"Now, don't go all sulky on me. How long have I got before the Guards get back with Buchan?"

Tomb's face went blank for a moment as he used the Sight. "They're just approaching the front door. I'd better go down and greet them. If you're sure you're all right now . . ."

"I'm fine."

"Then I'll see you in a while."

He turned and left the room quickly, before she could say anything else. Rowan heaved a quiet but vehement sigh of relief. She knew she shouldn't be so harsh with him, but that damned puppy dog routine of his was getting on her nerves. Always doing her little favours, so she'd have to say something nice to him . . . She got up off the bed, stripped off her nightgown, and reached for her clothes. She was looking forward to hearing Hawk and Fisher tell about what had happened at the Hellfire Club.

Everyone was back in their favourite chairs in the drawing room. Tomb handed round long, narrow glasses of his syrupy sherry, and everyone except Hawk accepted the wine with a smile. Hawk sat back in his chair and tried not to feel like a barbarian. There was a quiet moment as everyone else sipped at their drinks.

"Let's start with the Hellfire Club," said Rowan finally. "What did you think of them, Captain Hawk?"

"A bunch of amateurs, playing with magic and jumping at shadows," said Hawk bluntly. "No danger to anyone, except maybe themselves."

"But did you turn up any connection to the God Killings?" asked Tomb, sitting forward on the edge of his chair, as though anxious not to miss a syllable.

"Not really," said Fisher. "But we did come across something interesting. Before we were seconded to you, Hawk and I were investigating the murder of a sorcerer named Bode." She didn't miss the quickly stifled reactions from Buchan and Rowan at Bode's name, but carried on as though she hadn't noticed. "We didn't have time to find out who killed him, but we did discover that Bode had been hired by some unknown person to carry out a secret mission on the Street of Gods."

"Did he succeed in this mission?" said Tomb.

"We don't know," said Fisher. "We didn't find any evidence directly linking him to the God Killings, but we did discover that Bode had been experimenting with homunculi; that is, magically produced physical duplicates."

"Yes, yes," said Rowan impatiently. "We all know what a homunculus is."

Fisher gave Rowan a hard look that didn't faze the mystic a bit, and then continued. "Somehow, Bode invested one of these duplicates with all his rage and hate, and set it to guard his house against intruders. He called it the Dark Man. It was huge, muscular, and very nasty. It murdered at least four people that we know of. Hawk and I killed it."

"This is all very interesting," said Rowan, "but what has it got to do with the Hellfire Club? Or the God Killings?"

Fisher looked at Hawk to see if he'd like to continue with the story, but he was busy looking for some convenient receptacle into which he could surreptitiously empty his sherry glass. Fisher sighed quietly, and continued. "On our way back from studying the murder sites of the three dead Beings, we were attacked by a second Dark Man. We killed him. A third Dark Man tried to kill us at the Hellfire Club. We killed that one too."

For a long moment no one said anything. Tomb was frowning deeply. "Did you notice any differences between the three homunculi?"

"Yeah," said Fisher. "They're getting harder to kill."

"More than that," said Hawk, putting down his empty sherry glass. "They were all unnaturally strong, but the muscular development was different each time. There was no way it could have been the same body . . . and yet, each time we met, the Dark Man was much harder to deal with. It's as though he learns from his previous mistakes. I think there's one single mind controlling all the homunculi, jumping from body to body. It's also quite possible that there are more Dark Men out there somewhere, waiting for another chance at us."

The God Squad looked at each other. "Can you tell us anything about this sorcerer Bode?" said Rowan.

"Well," said Hawk, "apart from his having a mysterious mission on the Street of Gods at the same time as the Gods started dying, apparently he also gave Lord Arthur Sinclair the original inspiration for the Hellfire Club. Bode does seem to get around, doesn't he? Did any of you know him?"

Buchan nodded slowly. "I met him a few times, on the Street of Gods. Seemed a pleasant enough sort, though I never did find out what he was doing on the Street. I haven't seen him for some time."

"Was this before or after the God Killings began?" said Fisher.

"Before, I think," said Buchan.

"Did you ever meet his girlfriend?" said Hawk.

Buchan shook his head. "Didn't know he had one. Is she important?"

"Beats me," said Hawk. "Anyone else here know Bode?"

"I met him once or twice," said Rowan. "He was asking questions on the Street, so I checked him out, just to see what he was up to. We get all sorts down here, and it pays to be careful. He was a bit vague about what he was doing on the Street, but that's not unusual. He seemed harmless enough, so I let him be."

"What kind of questions was he asking?" said Fisher.

Rowan shrugged. "Questions about the Gods. Their powers, their backgrounds, things like that. The usual tourist stuff. And I didn't see any girlfriend, either."

Hawk sat quietly a moment, letting his thoughts settle. Bode was turning out to be an important link in the case, but they didn't really know anything about him. Perhaps he should contact the Guards in charge of the Bode killing, and have them send over all the papers found in Bode's house. Maybe there was something in them that would shed more light on the sorcerer. . . .

"Assuming all the homunculi have a single mind," said Tomb slowly, "the important question must be who is controlling them."

"Well, Bode, I would assume," said Rowan. "After all, the Dark Men are all versions of his own body. Perhaps he knew he was going to die, so he committed suicide and transferred his soul into one of the homunculi. That way he'd be free to continue with his mission. Whatever it is."

"Suicide?" said Fisher. "The cause of death was a single stab wound through the heart! If it was suicide, what happened to the knife?"

"That's a good point," said Buchan. "But if it isn't Bode, who is it?"

"Presumably the anonymous person who gave him his mission," said Hawk. "Whoever it is didn't want to be seen on the Street of Gods in person. Which suggests that somebody would have known him and recognised him."

"Or her," said Fisher. "Remember the girlfriend? That could have been our unknown person, emerging briefly from the shadows to give Bode new orders."

"This is getting complicated," said Buchan. "If we assume the Dark Men aren't really Bode, why are they still after Hawk and Fisher?"

"Because we're dangerous," said Hawk. "We're getting

closer to the truth, and the Dark Man knows it."

"Wait a minute," said Tomb. "We're overlooking something important. Did I understand you to say that the sorcerer Bode was killed in his own house? Why didn't his magic protect him?"

"Good question," said Hawk. "We don't know. When we got there, there was no trace of magic anywhere in the house; no wards, no booby traps, nothing."

"That's insane," said Tomb flatly. "Even after his death, the protective wards should still have been there. They usually have to be dismantled by another sorcerer. Dammit, every sorcerer has wards of some kind; you can't work without them."

"All right," said Hawk. "So it's crazy. Doesn't surprise me. The whole damn case is crazy."

"But it is definitely looking more and more like one case," said Fisher.

"It seems to me," said Buchan, "that we're not going to get anywhere until we can find out what Bode was doing here on the Street. That's got to be the key to everything."

"So it would seem," said Tomb. "In which case, it's fortunate I asked an acquaintance of mine to join us here this evening. I thought Hawk and Fisher ought to meet him. He's very knowledgeable about the Street of Gods. It's said that nothing happens on the Street that he doesn't know about, often before it happens."

"Oh, no," said Buchan. "You haven't. You haven't called *him* in, have you? Not Lacey?"

"Dirty little sneak," muttered Rowan.

"He serves a purpose," said Tomb firmly. He turned to Hawk and Fisher and smiled, almost apologetically. "In order to do our job here on the Street, we have to be in constant touch with everything that's going on. Given the nature of the Street of Gods, that can be rather difficult. Rowan and I both have the Sight, but there's a limit to how much ground we can cover. So we are forced to depend on various reliable sources for our information."

"Right," said Buchan. "Half our budget goes on bribe money."

"And most of that goes to Lacey," said Rowan.

"He's always proved most useful to us," said Tomb. "He has his own organization of informants and eavesdroppers. They bring him all the news, rumour, and gossip, and he puts it all together. He's predicted more trends, business deals, heresies, and conspiracies than all our other sources put together."

"He's also a nasty, repellent little creep, and he makes my skin crawl," said Rowan.

"We know the sort," said Hawk. "We use informants in our line of work, too."

"How much do you pay them?" asked Buchan.

Hawk grinned. "Isobel lets them live. They seem happy to settle for that."

"Anyway," said Tomb, "our man Lacey is waiting just down the hall. With your permission, I'll have him join us."

He looked around for objections, but no one said anything. Buchan clearly didn't give a damn, and Rowan was sulking. Tomb gestured sharply with his left hand, and the drawing room door swung open on its own.

"Do come in, Lacey. There's a good fellow!" said Tomb loudly.

There was a pause, and then a wide, fleshy figure appeared in the doorway, smiling ingratiatingly. He was better than average in height, but his great bulk made him look shorter. He moved slowly but with surprising grace, and something in the way he held himself suggested he was no stranger to violence, should it prove necessary. He had a round bland face, the main features of which were his small, dark eyes and constant smile. Fisher didn't like the smile. It looked practised. His hair was dark and greasy, plastered flat and parted neatly down the middle. Just looking at him, you knew immediately that you could trust him completely, provided you kept up the payments, but that the moment you ran out of money he'd disappear in an instant. The smile got worse the more you saw of it; the insincerity of it grated on the nerves like fingernails on a blackboard. All in all, Lacey was the kind of man you didn't want to shake hands with, in case some of his personality rubbed off on you.

"My dear Tomb, how nice to see you again. Looking well, as always. And your charming associates, Buchan and Rowan; two of my favourite people." His voice sounded exactly the way you'd expect it to. Soft and breathy and thoroughly oily. The kind of sound a toad would make if it was trying to sell you a horse that nobody wanted. "Always happy to be of service to you, my friends. Now then, I see we have guests present; Captains of our illustrious city Guard, no less. Will you honour me with your names, sir and madam?"

"Captain Hawk and Captain Fisher," said Hawk. "We're here on official business."

Something happened to Lacey's face. He didn't flinch and he didn't stop smiling, but his eyes were suddenly cold and watchful. He looked very much as though he'd like to see how far it was to the door but didn't quite dare look. Apparently even on the Street of Gods, people had heard of Hawk and Fisher.

"The renowned Captains Hawk and Fisher; an honour indeed to make your acquaintance. What can I do for you?"

"We need information," said Rowan. "Not long ago, a sorcerer named Bode appeared on the Street, asking questions about the Gods. What can you tell us about him?"

Lacey smiled like a decrepit cherub, lowered himself into the one remaining chair, and laced his fingers across his vast stomach. "Bode. Yes, I know that name." He paused a moment, to arrange his weight more comfortably, and the chair creaked loudly. He smiled about him pleasantly, and then began to speak without pause or hesitation, as though he'd only been waiting for permission to speak a piece he'd already prepared. For all Hawk knew, that might just be the case.

"Bode was a low-level sorcerer," said Lacey. "Mainly interested in alchemy and the production of homunculi. An expensive interest, which he supported through his extensive knowledge of pills and potions. He was well known in his field, but was never going to be anyone important. He lacked the drive, and the determination. He knew this, but it didn't seem to bother him. He was not, by all accounts, ambitious.

"He first appeared on the Street of Gods just over a month ago, asking questions about the powers and backgrounds of the Gods. Where they came from, what attributes they possessed, why people worshipped them—the usual tourist stuff. Unlike most tourists, however, Bode wasn't prepared to settle for the usual answers. He kept digging for more and more details, refusing to be put off, even when it was made clear to him that some of his questions were not appreciated by the Beings involved. He just pressed even harder for answers, putting things together, despite several quite specific warnings. He was either very brave, very stupid, or lacking in any sense of self-preservation.

"He died quite recently, at his home in the Northside. Accounts of the manner of his death seem confused, but all the accounts agree that the good Captains Hawk and Fisher were somehow involved. As investigating officers."

Lacey sat back in his chair, smiling serenely in a self-satisfied way. There was a long pause, as everyone digested the information he'd provided.

"Did anyone spot anything . . . unusual, about Bode?" Hawk asked carefully.

"Well, apart from what I've already told you, there were a few interesting occurences. Several times on the Street Bode was recognised by old friends, who went over to talk to him, as old friends do. It would appear that Bode was very short with them on these occasions. He wouldn't discuss his business, or what he was doing on the Street, and on some occasions even pretended not to know them. All of which was most unlike Bode. Perhaps he thought he was acting undercover, so to speak, but he'd made no effort to disguise himself."

"Did anyone ever see Bode looking . . . different?"

asked Fisher. "Larger, more muscular?"

Lacey looked at her sharply. "An interesting question, Captain. It is true that since Bode's death previously reliable sources have reported seeing Bode walking the Street of Gods again, looking . . . somehow different. Perhaps you can shed a little light on that, Captain?"

"Not right now," said Fisher. "According to some reports, Bode sometimes met his girlfriend on the Street. Can you tell us anything about her?"

"Unfortunately I have been able to learn very little about her, Captain. She appeared on only three occasions, each time heavily muffled under a cloak and hood. On the last occasion two of my associates tried to get a close look at her. They both died, right there on the Street."

Hawk leaned forward on his chair. "How did they die?"

"Natural causes, Captain. Heart attacks. Simultaneous heart attacks."

"Sorcery," said Fisher. Lacey inclined his head in agreement but said nothing.

"So," said Rowan, "we have a sorcerer and a sorceress on the Street of Gods, asking questions about the Beings. Questions the Beings don't want to answer. Perhaps that's why the Beings died; because they wouldn't answer the questions."

"Or because they did," said Buchan.

Fisher looked at him. "I'm not sure I follow that."

"I'm not sure I do myself," said Buchan. "What worries me is how the Beings died. You'd need a hell of a lot of power to overcome a Being on his own territory. You'd need a sorcerer the level of the High Warlock. And if someone like that was on the Street, we'd all know about it."

"Let's move away from Bode for a moment," said Tomb. "Lacey, what is the situation on the Street at present? How are the Beings reacting to the murders?"

"Badly, my dear friend. There's a great deal of unease on the Street, both inside and outside the temples. In their own way, the Beings are quite frightened. They all tend to paranoia at the best of times. Right now most of them are busy looking for an enemy they can blame everything on; someone to strike back at. Old rivalries are becoming more intense. Old hatreds are being fuelled afresh. Everyone knows you're doing your best to find the killer, but the Gods aren't known for their patience. I fear it's only a matter of time before some God decides to take matters into its own hands and strikes the first blow. And we all know what that would lead to."

"You're talking about a God War," said Tomb.

"Yes, I'm rather afraid I am. Unless something is done soon, something significant, things are going to get worse on the Street very quickly. As it is, we're all waiting for the inevitable spark to set off a conflagration none of us can hope to put out."

There was another long pause.

"I can't help feeling we're missing something," said Buchan. "Something so close we can't see the wood for the trees. Lacey, do you know of any connection between the three dead Beings?"

For the first time, Lacey looked a little uneasy, though his smile never wavered. "Well, there is one . . . coincidence, my friends, but it may be nothing more than that. . . ."

"We'll decide what's important," said Rowan sharply. "What is it?"

Lacey braced himself visibly. "Each of the dead Beings received a visit from the Deity Division, on official business, not long before their death."

Hawk looked sharply at Tomb. "Is that right?"

"Well, yes. But we visit Beings all the time. It's part of our job. We've visited so many Beings recently, I hadn't even noticed the dead Beings were included."

"But it is a connection," said Fisher.

And then the voice of the Guard's communications sorcerer boomed suddenly in Hawk and Fisher's minds:

Riot on the Street of Gods! Riot on the Street of Gods! All available personnel report to the Street of Gods immediately. This command overrides all other orders and priorities until further notice.

Hawk and Fisher scrambled to their feet, their hands clawing instinctively for their weapons. The God Squad were on their feet too, looking equally shocked. They'd picked up the message, too. Lacey rose uncertainly to his feet.

"My friends, what is it? What has happened?"

"It seems your information came a little too late this time," said Rowan. "Someone's just fired the first shot in a God War."

She ran out of the door, with Tomb close behind her. Lacey made as though to approach Buchan, and then hesitated.

"Pardon my intrusion, my friends, but about my fee . . ."

"Worry about that later," said Hawk. "Buchan . . ."

"But . . ."

"I said later!" Hawk glared at Lacey, and the informer backed quickly away. Hawk turned back to Buchan, who was still standing in a daze. "I think we ought to get moving, sir Buchan. The riot won't wait for us to get there."

"Of course. I'm sorry. I just never really thought it would happen, that's all. There hasn't been a serious riot on the Street in almost seventy years."

"Seventy-one," said Lacey. No one paid any attention.

"You're the expert," Hawk said to Buchan. "What's the best thing to do?"

"Pray," said Buchan. "But make sure you pick the right God."

Hawk could hear the riot long before he could see it. Screams of rage and horror and anguish blended into a rising cacophony of sound that permeated the night air. The Street of Gods felt strangely out of synch, as though the various realities that made it up were no longer in alignment. Churches appeared and disappeared, and doors changed shape. Unnatural lights blazed in the starless sky, spread across the night like colors on a madman's palette. A surging vibration trembled in the ground underfoot, like the slow, regular heartbeat of something indescribably huge, buried down below.

Hawk and Fisher ran down the Street, weapons at the ready. They'd been running for some time, but the riot didn't seem to be getting any nearer. The Street was like that, sometimes, but at that moment it wasn't doing a thing for Hawk's nerves. He breathed deeply, trying to get more air into his lungs, and hoped his second wind would kick in soon. Fisher seemed to be struggling a little too, and she could usually run him into the ground. Buchan, on the other hand, was loping effortlessly along beside them, as though he covered this kind of distance every day before breakfast and thought nothing of it. With his physique, maybe he did. Hawk tried to stick with that train of thought, but his mind insisted on bringing him back to what passed for reality on the Street of Gods. The Guard communications sorcerer hadn't been very specific about how bad the riot was, but he wouldn't have sent out a general alarm like that unless his superiors had been sure something extremely nasty was happening up ahead.

He wondered briefly where Tomb and Rowan were. They'd disappeared even before Hawk had left God Squad headquarters, but there was no sign of them on the Street. Maybe they knew a shortcut. Maybe they'd already got to the riot, and had things safely under control. *Yeah*, thought Hawk sourly, *and while I'm wishing, I'd like a fortune in jewels as well, please*. The constant roar of noise was growing louder, uglier and more violent by the minute. Hawk rounded a corner that hadn't been there the last time he'd been this way, and then skidded to a halt, Fisher and Buchan piling up beside him. They'd found the riot.

Hundreds, maybe thousands of gaudily robed priests and acolytes were milling back and forth on the Street, furiously attacking each other with swords and fists and broken bottles. Everywhere there were bloody hands and faces, and unmoving bodies were being trampled blindly underfoot by the savage mob. Old hatreds were running loose and free, as age-old vendettas finally came to a head. Blinding lights flared from churches and temples, and overhead the sky churned sickly with uncontrolled magic. A handful of Guards had got there before Hawk and Fisher, and were fighting back to back on the edges of the crowd, too busy trying to stay alive to do anything about the riot. The Street belonged to the fanatics now, and they didn't care who they killed. A dozen green-robed priests swarmed over a Guard Constable and knocked him to the ground. He disappeared behind a host of swinging boots.

Hawk and Fisher waded in to help. Whatever else was happening, Guards looked after their own. They had to. No one else would. Hawk's axe swept back and forth in short, vicious arcs, and blood flew on the air. The priests scattered, and Fisher cut down those who didn't move fast enough. No one attacked a Guard and got away with it. It might give people ideas. The remaining priests disappeared into the crowd, and Buchan stood guard as Hawk and Fisher got the battered Constable to his feet and led him to the safety of a recessed doorway. There was blood on his face and his legs were shaky, but he seemed more or less intact. He nodded his thanks, and tried to get his thoughts together.

"Have you been here long?" asked Hawk.

"Can't be more than ten, twenty minutes," said the Constable breathlessly. "But it seems like forever. Just my luck to be working a beat so close to the Street of Gods when the riot call came. . . . "

"Do you know what caused all this?" said Fisher.

"Seems another God has been murdered," said the Constable. He paused to wipe blood out of his eyes. Buchan passed him an immaculately clean handkerchief, and the Constable pressed it gingerly to his forehead. "The Lord of the New Flesh is dead. Someone ripped both its hearts right out of its breast. The High Priest found the body less than an hour ago. Didn't take long for word to get around. We don't know who actually started the riot. Could have been anybody."

"Details can wait," said Fisher. "How many more Guards are there already here?"

"There were seventeen. We all got here about the same time, but the crowd separated us. We'd better get some reinforcements here soon. The Beings are mad as hell and scared spitless. It's only a matter of time before one of them decides to take a hand personally. And you can bet your arse if one God comes out onto the Street, they all bloody will. Where the hell's the God Squad? They're supposed to prevent things like this from happening!"

"They're here somewhere," said Hawk, carefully not looking at Buchan. "We'll just have to try and keep the lid on things until they get their act together. Has anybody sent for the SWAT team?"

The Guard smiled sourly. "First thing we did when we got here was to scream for the SWAT team. But according to the communications sorcerer, they're busy dealing with an emergency on the other side of the city. Typical. They're never bloody around when they're needed. We need them here! We can't cope with this!"

"Take it easy," said Fisher. "We're just Guards, not heroes. No one expects us to cope with everything. We just do the best we can." She broke off to wave urgently at a contingent of Guards running down the Street toward them. "Look; you join up with this bunch, and fill them in on the situation. We'll do what we can here. Now move it!"

The Constable nodded briefly, and moved off to intercept the newcomers. Hawk and Fisher looked at the growing riot, and then at Buchan.

"If it was up to me," said Hawk, "I'd just let them get on with it. With a bit of luck all the fanatics would kill each other off and the Street of Gods would be a far more peaceful place. But, unfortunately, the Constable was right. If we don't break this up, the Gods will get involved. And if that happens, I for one am not hanging around to see who wins. I am going to beg, borrow, or steal a pair of fast horses, and you can wave Fisher and me goodbye as we head for the nearest horizon."

Buchan looked at Fisher. "He really would, wouldn't he?"

"No," said Fisher. "He's not that sensible. He always did think about his duty too damned much. And since I won't leave without him, it looks like we're here for the duration." She looked out over the frenzied mob and shook her head disgustedly. "I've seen smaller armies. You're the expert, Buchan. How do we handle this?"

"Clear the Street," said Buchan firmly. "Don't worry about the Gods; Tomb and Rowan will take care of them if necessary. The rioters are our responsibility."

"Get everyone off the Street," said Hawk. "Just like that?"

"It's not difficult," said Buchan. "We just have to make them more scared of us than they are of anything else. They may look dangerous, but most of them aren't armed, and those who are probably don't have much combat experience. Either way, they're no match for professionals like us."

Hawk looked at him steadily. "So we just wade right in and slaughter everything that moves. Is that it?"

"Pretty much," said Buchan. "And watch yourselves; rioting is a capital offence, and they know it. They'll kill you if you give them an opening. Don't make the mistake of thinking they'll respond to reason. They won't. They're beyond that now. So just do what you have to do, and worry about the body count later."

He walked unhurriedly into the riot, and his sword flashed. Robed bodies fell to the ground and didn't move again.

"The trouble is, he's right," said Hawk. "I hate this job sometimes."

"If we don't stop this riot, hundreds will die," said Fisher. "Maybe thousands. What are a few lives, compared to that?"

"I know," said Hawk. "But it doesn't make it any easier. I joined the Guard to protect people, not butcher them. Come on, lass. Let's do it."

Fisher nodded, and together they moved silently into the riot and began the slaughter. They worked back to back,

blades swinging, and blood splashed their cloaks. Robes
of all shapes and colors surged around Hawk, the fanatics
nothing more than angry faces and flailing fists. A few had
swords. Some had clubs and lengths of chain. None of them
stood a chance against Hawk and Fisher. Hawk swung his
axe back and forth in wide, brutal arcs, and bodies crumpled
to every side of him. Fisher guarded his back, her blade a
silver blur as men and women fell screaming to the ground.
The crowd began to fall back around them, and some of the
rioters turned to flee rather than face the grim-faced Guards.

More Guards spilled onto the Street of Gods from all
directions, drawn from all over the city, and soon the cobbled ground was slippery with blood and gore. An armoured
contingent arrived from the Brotherhood of Steel, eager for
a fight and determined to restore order. The sound of the
crowd changed, fear replacing rage, and it began to crumble
and fall apart under the onslaught of so many determined
professional fighting men. Priests and acolytes threw down
their weapons and ran for the safety of their temples. Piles
of dead and injured lay scattered across the Street, mostly
ignored. Some of them were Guards. A handful of Guard
sorcerers appeared on the scene, and slowly the shifting
realities returned to what passed for normal on the Street
of Gods.

Hawk slowly lowered his axe and looked about him, pant-
ing for breath. The Street was emptying fast, and a slow sul-
len silence had fallen across the night. Tired-looking Guards
were sorting the injured rioters from the dead, and finishing
the job. Rioting, as Buchan had said, was a capital offence.
Hawk turned his head away, and sat down suddenly, his
back to a wall. There were some things he wouldn't do,
and to hell with what the law said. Fisher sat down beside
him, and leaned against him, her head on his shoulder.

"They're not paying us enough for this," she said indis-
tinctly.

"They couldn't pay us enough for this," said Hawk.

"Then why are we doing it?"

"Because someone has to protect the innocent and avenge

the wronged. It's a matter of honour. And duty."

"That argument doesn't sound as convincing as it used to."

Hawk nodded slowly. "At least the worst is over now."

A harsh metallic scream broke the silence, deafeningly loud and utterly inhuman. Hawk and Fisher scrambled to their feet and looked round just in time to see something huge and deadly surging out of a temple doorway not nearly big enough to let it through. Stone and timber broke apart and fell away as the Being emerged onto the Street of Gods. It was at least thirty feet high, a shimmering patchwork of metal fragments held together by rags and strings of rotting flesh. Patches of dark, discolored skin revealed splintered bone and obscurely connected metal mechanisms. Steel and crystal machine parts thrust through the tattered hide, their razor-sharp edges grinding together as the Being rose to its full height. A roaring crimson fire burned in its steel belly and glowed in its bony eye sockets.

It had slender jagged arms with long-clawed hands that shimmered in its own bloody light. Broken silver chains hung from its wrists. Its steel jaws snapped together like a man-trap. A long tail studded with bony spikes lashed back and forth behind it. The Being threw back its long, wedge-shaped head and screamed defiance at the night. It had got out, and there was nothing anyone could do to stop it. It screamed again, a harsh metallic shriek that sent a sudden shiver through Hawk. There was nothing remotely human in the sound. The creature should never have lived, and was not alive in any way that made sense. But this was the Street of Gods, and it had got out, and not even those who had prayed to it for so long could hope to control it now.

It lowered its massive head, and looked at the Guards and Brothers of Steel gathered before it. There were close on three hundred armed men facing the Being, and Hawk knew with a sickening certainty that they weren't going to be enough. The huge creature darted forward, and its razor-sharp claws raked through a dozen men. More died screaming as the creature surged back and forth, crushing men

under its massive bulk. Swords and axes cut uselessly at
the Being's patchwork hide. Its long head snapped down
to bite a man in half. Blood dripped from the metal jaws
like steaming saliva. The Guards and the Brotherhood fell
back, only their training keeping them from utter panic. The
few Guard sorcerers roared and chanted, but their magics
shattered harmlessly against the rogue Being, whose very
existence defied the laws of reality.

"Where the hell did that thing come from?" said Fisher,
as she and Hawk peered warily at the creature from the
shadows of a concealed doorway.

"Must be a God of some kind," said Hawk.

"You mean there are people crazy enough to worship
that?"

"This is Haven, Isobel; they'll worship bloody anything
here. And if one God's out, it won't be long before more
come out to join it. I think this might be a good time to
make a strategic retreat."

Fisher looked at him sharply. "We're not going anywhere,
Hawk. We're God Squad now. And since the rest of the
Squad has apparently vanished, that means that thing is our
responsibility. It has to be stopped here, before it gets into
a more populated part of the city."

Hawk scowled. "I hate it when you're right. Okay; you
take left, I'll take right. We'll circle round behind the thing
and see if we can cut through whatever it has instead of
tendons in its legs. That should bring it down to our height
if nothing else."

"And if that doesn't work?"

"Pray really hard that Tomb and Rowan are on their way
here, instead of doing the sensible thing and hiding in a
storm cellar somewhere."

"You worry too much, Hawk. After all, we've faced
worse, in our time."

They shared a smile, and then separated, darting silently
from shadow to shadow as they made their way behind the
unliving creature. The Being reared up to its full height and
glared down at the Guards and Brothers of Steel scattered

around it. It screamed again, the inhuman sound echoing
on and on. The sound was almost painfully loud as Hawk
emerged from the shadows behind the Being, hefting his
axe. Up close, the dead flesh smelt of corruption and burning oil. The Being's leg was taller than Hawk and easily twice as broad. There were flat plates of metal sliding
against each other, and fraying ropes of muscle that flexed
and tore with every movement. Steel cables stretched and
hummed, lined with traceries of broken veins. Hawk looked
at the axe in his hand and shook his head slowly.

This is probably a really bad idea. . . .

He gripped the axe firmly with both hands, and swung
it with all his strength at one of the steel cables in the left
leg. The heavy axe sheared clean through the cable, and
wedged itself between the moving parts inside the leg. The
Being screamed deafeningly. Hawk tugged at his axe, but
it was stuck tight. The Being lifted its leg, and Hawk was
jerked up into the air, still clinging grimly to his axe. The
foot slammed down heavily, cracking the cobbled ground,
and Hawk was thrown clear. He lay on his back a moment,
dazed, and then rolled quickly to one side. The taloned foot
slammed down where he'd been lying. He clambered shakily to his feet, and saw his axe protruding from the leg, just
in front of him. He grabbed it firmly with both hands, pulled
hard, and almost fell down again as it came away easily.
The impact of the stamping foot had jarred it loose.

Great, thought Hawk, circling quickly to keep behind the
Being. *Now what do I do? Cutting the cable didn't even
slow the bloody thing down.*

He caught a glimpse of something moving on the edge
of his vision. He spun round, axe at the ready, and then
relaxed a little as he saw it was Fisher. He just had time to
nod acknowledgement, and then both of them had to throw
themselves to the ground as a huge clawed hand slashed
through the air where they'd been a moment before. They hit
the ground rolling and were up and running before the Being
could turn to face them. They ran in different directions to
confuse it, but the huge creature paused only briefly before

going after Fisher. Hawk swore briefly, and running after the Being, cut at one of its legs with his axe to get the creature's attention. The great wedge head swung down toward him, full of bloody steel teeth over a foot long. Hawk threw himself between the creature's legs and pounded down the Street after Fisher. The Being screamed deafeningly, and started after them.

The two Guards darted into a narrow alleyway, and the Being lurched to a halt at the alley mouth, uncertain how to get at them. Hawk and Fisher backed away down the alley, not taking their eyes off the creature. And then it slowly turned its head and looked away, as though sensing a greater menace close at hand. It looked back down the Street, and turned quickly to face the new threat. Hawk and Fisher watched silently from the protective shadows.

Tomb and Rowan were standing side by side in the middle of the Street of Gods, facing the rogue Being. Everyone else had disappeared. Only the dead remained, scattered over the cobbles like so many crumpled heaps of bloody clothing. The Being stared at Tomb and Rowan with its furnace eyes, and then started slowly, deliberately, toward them. Rowan held up her left hand. A small blue jewel blazed brightly in her grasp, the azure light spilling between her fingers. The Exorcist Stone. Rowan spoke a single Word of Power, and in a moment that seemed to last forever, the world changed.

Reality convulsed, shaking like a plucked harp string, and the rogue Being was suddenly no longer there. There was a sharp clap of thunder as air rushed in to fill the vacuum left by its sudden disappearance. And as quickly as that, it was all over. The night air was still and quiet, and the Street of Gods was calm again. Tomb and Rowan turned away as the Guards and Brothers of Steel reappeared on the Street and moved among them, doing what they could to help the injured. The Exorcist Stone had disappeared, tucked casually away into one of Rowan's pockets.

Hawk and Fisher leaned wearily back against the wall at the alley mouth, eyes closed, letting their aching muscles slowly relax. Tiredness so deep it was more like pain coursed through Hawk's body, tugging at his muscles like a persistent beggar demanding attention.

"So," he said finally. "That was the Exorcist Stone."

"Yeah," said Fisher. "Impressive. Pretty color, too."

"If nothing else, it should calm things down a bit. Both the Beings and their priests will think twice before getting out of line again."

"Don't bank on it," said Fisher. "That's too sensible, too logical. Nothing on this bloody Street is ever logical."

"True."

They moved out onto the Street of Gods to help with the injured. Tomb waved and smiled at them briefly, but he and Rowan were too busy to break away. Buchan appeared from among a group of Guards, caught Hawk and Fisher's attention, and strode quickly toward them. Hawk took in Buchan's face and stance, and his heart sank. Whatever the man had to say, Hawk knew instinctively he didn't want to hear it. Buchan came to a halt before Hawk and Fisher, and nodded briskly. There was blood on his clothes and hands, none of it his.

"Whatever it is, the answer's no," said Hawk flatly. "I don't care if someone's planning to destroy the whole Street of Gods. I might even applaud. Isobel and I are exhausted. We've worked too hard too long, and we're way behind on our sleep. That's a dangerous state to be in. It's too easy to make mistakes when you're tired. So, Isobel and I are going to help out here for a while, and then we're going home to get some sleep. Whatever you want will just have to wait."

"Right," said Fisher.

"Sleep can wait," said Buchan. "This can't. I was just talking to one of the Guard sorcerers. Something nasty is building at Hightower Hall. Something really nasty. Tomb and Rowan can't go. They're needed here. That just leaves us."

"Read my lips," said Hawk. "We're not going. Isobel's out on her feet and I'm not much better. If the Hellfire Club's got their fingers burnt, it's their own damned fault."

"This is God Squad business," said Buchan. "We can't turn our back on people who need us just because we don't like them."

"Watch me. Isobel's in no state . . . "

"Oh, hell, let's go," said Fisher. "The time we spend arguing with Buchan, we could be there and back. Besides, I haven't got the strength to argue."

"That's the spirit," said Buchan. "It's only a mile or so to High Tory from here. We can do it in ten minutes if we hurry. Don't you just love working in the God Squad? Never a dull moment."

He set off briskly down the Street of Gods, and Hawk and Fisher moved wearily after him.

"If he doesn't stop being so bloody cheerful," growled Hawk ominously, "I am personally going to tie both his legs in a square knot."

"I'll help," said Fisher.

They hurried after Buchan, muttering mutinously under their breath. From the shadows of a side alley, the Dark Man watched them go but made no move to follow.

6

Needs, Desires, And Other Motives

By the time they reached Hightower Hall, Hawk had found his second wind and was feeling only moderately shattered. The crisp cold air of winter felt refreshing after the close, humid warmth of the Street of Gods, and helped to clear his head. Even so, it was Buchan who noticed the first sign of something amiss. He stopped well short of the tall iron gates and looked uncertainly about him. Hawk and Fisher stopped with him, their hands dropping automatically to their weapons.

"What's wrong?" said Fisher.

"It's too quiet," said Buchan slowly. "And there's no one watching the gates. Where are all the men-at-arms? They wouldn't just go off and leave the gates unguarded." He reached out and pushed at the gates, and they swung slowly open at the pressure. "Not even locked. Something unexpected must have happened. An emergency, a call for help; something. The men-at-arms went to investigate . . . and never came back." He looked slowly around him, senses straining and alert. "There's something else too; a feeling on the air . . . "

Hawk nodded. He could feel it prickling on his skin and scratching at his nerves; a vague pressure, like the building tension on the air that warns of an approaching storm. "Magic," he said flatly. "The Hellfire Club finally found a ritual that worked."

He hefted his axe once, and then moved cautiously through the gates and into the grounds. The only light came from the half-moon overhead and the wide blazing windows of the Hall. All was still and quiet. There was no sign of men-at-arms anywhere. Hawk padded softly forward, Fisher and Buchan close behind him, swords at the ready. They walked on the grass, avoiding the gravel pathway. Gravel was noisy. The Hall loomed up ahead, silhouetted against the night sky.

Almost halfway there, Hawk found two of the guard dogs. They were lying stretched out on the grass, still and silent, two darker shadows in the gloom. Hawk knelt down beside them, and pushed one gently with his fingertips. The body rolled slightly back and forth, and then was still again. Both dogs were dead. He checked them over quickly, but there was no sign of any wound, no trace to show what had killed them. It was as though they'd just lay down where they were, and the life went out of them.

"Captain Fisher," said Buchan quietly. "Do you still have your suppressor stone?"

"Sure," said Fisher. "Why?"

"Activate it. Now. And you and Captain Hawk had better stay close together. That way, the stone will protect you both from any general magic in the area."

"What about you?" said Hawk.

"I have my own stone," said Buchan. "Now let's get moving. Something bad has happened at the Hall, and I have a horrible feeling we've got here too late to stop it."

He and Fisher muttered over their suppressor stones, and then the three of them moved warily forward into the darkness, their eyes fixed on the Hall. There was still no sign of any movement at the brightly blazing windows. Hawk was the first to reach the front door. It was open,

standing slightly ajar. Hawk pushed at it with his foot.
The door moved back a way, and then stopped as it hit
an obstruction. Hawk eased himself through the narrow
gap and looked down to see what was blocking the door.
As he'd expected, it was a body: one of the men-at-arms.
Hawk knelt down and checked quickly for vital signs.
The man-at-arms was alive, but only just. His skin was
cold and deathly pale, his pulse slow, and his breathing
disturbingly shallow. Hawk straightened up and looked
along the hallway. More men-at-arms lay scattered and
unmoving the length of the entrance hall. Hawk squeezed
through the doorway, followed by Fisher and Buchan.

"There was an emergency," said Buchan quietly. "Someone called for help. The men-at-arms came running, from
the house and from the grounds. This was as far as they got.
Whatever the Hellfire Club has called up, it didn't want to
be disturbed."

"But how could they have called up something?" said
Fisher. "They were a bunch of amateurs; you said so yourself."

"They must have had help."

Hawk frowned. "What kind of help?"

"Good question," said Buchan. "Let's go and find out."

He took the lead, and guided Hawk and Fisher unerringly
through the maze of corridors that led to the ballroom. The
silence was complete, broken only by their own soft footsteps. They found servants here and there, lying crumpled
where they fell, struck down by the same deathly sleep.
Hawk peered continuously about him, skin crawling in
anticipation of the attack that never came, his tiredness
burned away by rising adrenalin.

They finally came to the closed double doors that led to
the ballroom. Buchan made as though to push the doors
open and walk straight in, but Hawk stopped him with a
cautious hand on his arm. He looked warily around him,
then stepped forward, and pressed his ear against the right-
hand door. He couldn't hear anything. Either the wood was
too thick, or there wasn't anything to hear. Taking hold of

both door-handles, he very carefully eased the doors open an inch or two and then stepped back. He made sure his grip on his axe was secure, looked quickly at Fisher and Buchan, then stepped forward and kicked the doors open. The three of them surged forward to fill the doorway, weapons at the ready.

The Quality lay strewn across the waxed and polished floor of the ballroom in their brightly colored finery, like so many broken butterflies. They lay singly or in heaps, wherever they'd been standing when the magic struck them down. Most were awake but unable to move. Some were moaning quietly, as much in horror as in pain. All of them looked withered and ancient, aged long beyond their years, held somehow on the very edge of death as their life drained slowly out of them. Those nearest the blue chalk circle looked almost mummified. And there, in the middle of the ballroom, inside the blue circle, stood the thing the Hellfire Club had called up out of the Gulfs. It looked across at the doorway, and smiled charmingly.

"Well, now," it said in a soft, pleasant voice. "Visitors. How nice."

The figure was six feet tall, quite naked, and aesthetically muscular in a way usually achieved only by statues. Its face was classically handsome and unmarked by time, so flawlessly perfect as to be almost inhuman. A raw sensuality burned around it like an invisible flame, attractive and repellent in its uncaring arrogance, like bitter honey or the smell of an open wound masked by perfume. It was the perfect embodiment of the male form, burning with ruthless vitality.

"What's wrong with the Quality?" said Fisher softly. "What's happened to them?"

"The creature they called up is draining the life right out of them," said Buchan. "Their deaths will make it even more powerful. Even a low-level sorcerer would have known to set wards so this couldn't happen, but these people were amateurs, and they didn't know. At least they had enough sense to draw a restraining circle. That should hold it for a while."

"How long?" said Hawk, not taking his gaze from the figure before him.

"Only as long as it takes to drain its summoners dry," said Buchan. "After that, it'll be powerful enough to break the circle, and there'll be nothing we can do to stop it."

"What about the Exorcist Stone?" said Fisher.

Buchan smiled tiredly. "The creature will be gone long before we could get the Stone here, and all the Quality will be dead."

"Great," said Hawk. "Just great." He moved slowly forward, stopping right at the edge of the chalk circle. The creature watched him intently, still smiling its perfect smile. Hawk looked into its dark unblinking eyes and saw no humour there, or any other emotion he could recognise. "Who are you?" he said harshly. "What are you?"

"I'm what they wanted," said the thing in the circle. "I'm all the darkness in their souls, all their hidden hates and wants and desires set free at last, given shape and form and substance, in me. I'm strong and beautiful and perfect because that's what they wanted me to be. Or perhaps because that's how they see themselves, in the privacy of their mind's eye. It really doesn't matter. They gave me life, whether they meant to or not, and they'll go on giving me life until they die. Then, when I have fully come into my power, I'll leave them here and go out into the city. A new Being, in all his glory. A new God for the Street of Gods. And men shall worship me as they always have, under one name or another, in blood and suffering and all the hidden darkness of their souls. I shall be very happy here. This city was built with me in mind."

"I've met your kind before," said Hawk. "You're just another Dark Man with delusions of grandeur, that's all."

"I shall show you blood and horror," said the creature pleasantly. "I will break your body and your spirit, and you will praise me before I let you die. You don't understand what I am. What I really am. I'm everything that ever scared

you, every dark impulse you tried to hide, your worst night-
mare given flesh and blood and bone."

"You're also stuck in that circle," said Fisher, moving
forward to stand beside Hawk. "And if you had any power
to use against us, you'd have used it by now. You're not
leaving this circle. You're not going anywhere. We'll see
to that."

"So brave," said the creature. "And so foolish. You are
nothing compared to me."

Fisher grinned. "Fancies himself, doesn't he? Let's see
how he likes half a yard of cold steel rammed through his
appendix."

"No!" said Buchan, moving quickly forward to join the
two Guards at the edge of the circle. "Don't try it, Captain.
You can't reach the thing from outside the circle, and once
you cross the chalk line your suppressor stone wouldn't be
able to protect you anymore. The creature would drain you
dry just like the Quality."

"No problem," said Fisher. She sheathed her sword, took
a throwing knife from her left boot, aimed and let fly with
a single rapid movement. The creature's hand moved, too
quickly for the eye to follow, and snatched the knife in mid-
air. It dropped the knife to the floor and smiled at Fisher.
She blinked, and turned to Buchan. "We might just have a
problem here after all. How long do you think we've got
before it has enough power to leave the circle?"

"Not long. Half the Quality are at death's door already.
Whatever we're going to do, we've got to do it soon."

"Wait a minute," said Hawk. "The Exorcist Stone would
get rid of it, right? How about the suppressor stone? That's
supposed to work on the same principle, isn't it?"

Buchan frowned. "Well, yes, but it's nowhere near as
powerful. You'd have to get the suppressor stone within an
inch or so of the creature, and even then there's no guarantee it would work. And if it didn't . . . the creature would
either drain you like the Quality, or tear you apart just for
the fun of it."

"If we wait till it gets out of the circle we're dead anyway," said Hawk. "Look, if you've got a better idea, let's hear it. I'm not actually wild about going into that bloody circle unless I have to."

"There is . . . another alternative," said Buchan. He turned his back on the creature and looked out over the ballroom. "It's gathering its power from the life force of the quality. If they were all to die—before the creature could come into its full power—it would remain helpless within the circle."

"We can't just kill them!" said Hawk.

"It's inhuman!" said Fisher. "We can't!"

"You think I like suggesting it?" snapped Buchan. "I grew up with these people! They're my friends!"

"It's out of the question," said Hawk flatly.

"No it isn't," said a quiet voice from among the Quality. "Kill us. Kill us all. Please. Do you think we want to live like this?"

They found Lord Louis Hightower sitting propped up against the wall. His flesh was pale and blotched and heavily wrinkled, sunk right back to the bone, and Buchan only recognised him by his clothes. His mouth was just a colorless gash, and his breathing barely stirred his chest, but still he fought to force out his words as Buchan knelt beside him.

"If we die, the shock will kill that thing. It's linked to us."

"Louis . . . "

"Do it, Charles! Please. I can't face living like this."

"No!" said Hawk. "If we can kill the thing while it's still in the circle, there's a damn good chance you'll get your life back. The link between you works both ways. Or it should." He knelt down beside the mummified figure. "Let us at least try to save you. I've lost two Hightowers already. I don't want to lose a third."

Hightower looked at him, and his mouth moved in something that might have been a smile. "All right, Captain. Go ahead. But, this time, get it right."

Hawk nodded stiffly, then straightened up and headed

back to the edge of the circle. Fisher and Buchan went with
him.

"I take it you do have some kind of plan," said Buchan.

"I wouldn't bank on it," said Fisher. "Hawk's always
been a great one for improvising."

"Well, basically, I thought I'd cut the creature's heart
out and jam the suppressor stone into the hole," said Hawk.
"That should ruin its day."

"Sounds good to me," said Fisher. "You hit him from
the left, I'll hit him from the right."

"This is crazy," said Buchan. "Absolutely bloody crazy.
Let's do it, before we get an attack of common sense and
change our minds."

The three of them spread out round the circle, weapons at
the ready. The creature smiled at them warmly and spread its
arms as though welcoming them. Hawk hesitated a moment
at the chalk line, then braced himself and stepped quickly
across it. The years hit him like a club, almost forcing
him to his knees. He could feel his joints stiffening and
his muscles shrivelling as life itself was sucked out of him
to feed the creature before him. His axe grew heavier with
every movement, and it took all his strength to keep his
back straight and his head erect. He heard shocked gasps
of pain and horror as Fisher and Buchan entered the circle,
but he didn't look round. He didn't want to see what was
happening to them. He didn't want to think about what was
happening to him. He hefted his axe, and threw himself at
the smiling creature.

It dodged the axe easily, and sent Hawk flying across
the circle with a casual backhand blow. He hit the ground
hard, driving the breath from his lungs, and for a moment
he couldn't find the strength to get to his knees. He gritted
his teeth and staggered to his feet again, swaying from the
effort. Fisher and Buchan were cutting at the creature with
their swords, but the thing simply raised its arms to ward
off the blows, and the blades sprang away as though they'd
met solid metal instead of flesh. The creature's arms weren't
even bruised.

Fisher was an old woman, with white hair and a heavily lined face. Buchan was bent and twisted with age, barely able to hold onto his sword. Hawk fought down a rising tide of panic. Their weapons were no use against the creature, but they had nothing else. Except the suppressor stones. *Get the stone close to him.* That was what Buchan had said. *Get it as close as possible, or it won't work.* Hawk scowled. He knew what he'd like to do with the stone. . . . The scowl slowly became a smile. When in doubt, be direct. He waited a moment as Buchan and Fisher gathered up their remaining strength and threw themselves at the creature, and then he put away his axe and lurched forward. The creature saw him coming, but since Hawk was empty-handed, ignored him to concentrate on fending off its armed attackers. Hawk moved in behind the creature, took a deep breath, and jumped the thing from behind, locking an arm round the creature's throat. It tried to grab him to throw him off, but couldn't quite reach. Hawk hung on grimly, forcing the head back.

"Isobel!" he yelled harshly. "Get the stone and ram it down his throat!"

Fisher dropped her sword and clawed the suppressor stone from her pocket. Buchan leapt forward and grabbed both the creature's arms. Fisher seized the creature's chin, yanked it down, and pressed the stone into its mouth. Then she forced the mouth closed with both hands and held on with all her strength. The creature bucked and heaved and threw Hawk off. Buchan let go its arms, stepped back a pace, and punched the creature in the throat. It gagged, swallowed despite itself, and then screamed horribly. There was a small, very localized explosion, and then Hawk, Fisher, and Buchan were alone in the circle.

Hawk blinked dazedly a moment, then looked at Fisher, and smiled widely with relief. She was herself again, the added years gone along with the creature that had tried to force them on her. They hugged each other tightly for a long moment, and then let go and looked around them. There was a rising hum of voices as the Quality discovered that they also had been renewed. Buchan was already moving among them, grinning and laughing and being slapped on the back. Fisher noticed that her sword, her knife, and the suppressor stone were lying on the floor inside the circle, and she bent down to retrieve them.

"One of your better ideas, Hawk," she said finally, as she sheathed her sword. "Where did the creature go, do you suppose?"

Hawk shrugged. "Back where it came from. And good riddance."

The noise in the ballroom had risen from a babble to a roar, as the Quality tried to figure out what had happened, and exactly who was to blame. Lord Hightower shook Buchan firmly by the hand, and then strode over to join the two Guards. He nodded to them both, and they bowed politely.

"I just wanted to extend my personal thanks and congratulations. I'll see there's a commendation in this for both of you. Going into that circle after the creature was the bravest thing I've ever seen."

"Thank you, my Lord," said Hawk. "It's all part of the job."

"I didn't get a chance to talk to you the last time you were here. I wanted to assure you and your partner that I don't hold you in any way responsible for the deaths of my father or my brother Paul. I checked you out very thoroughly. It wasn't your fault. You mustn't blame yourselves."

"Thank you," said Hawk. "I'm glad you feel that way. I never really had the chance to know your father, but I liked your brother. He was a good man to work with."

"Speaking of blame," said Buchan, as he joined them, "How the hell did you manage to raise that creature in the first place?"

Hightower frowned unhappily. "Lord Brunel came into possession of an old grimoire, and persuaded us that some of its rituals might be adapted to suit our purposes. Yes, I know. We should have known better. But we thought we'd be safe, as long as we stayed outside the circle. . . . "

"Oh, that's typical, that is! Put all the blame on me!" Brunel's voice blared out from nearby, and the small group turned to see him stalking toward them. "You're not laying the blame for all this at my door. We discussed whether or not to use the ritual, and everyone agreed. Including you, Hightower. It wasn't my fault everything went wrong."

"We can talk about this later," said Buchan. "In the meantime, I think you'd better let me have the grimoire for safekeeping. My colleagues in the God Squad will want to examine it."

Brunel's hand dropped halfway to a square bulge underneath his waistcoat. "I'm not handing over anything. The grimoire's mine. If I let you have it I'll never see it again. I know your sort. You'd keep it for yourself. But you're not having it. There's power in this book, and it belongs to your betters. All right, things got a bit out of hand this time, but . . . "

"This time?" said Buchan. "You're not thinking of trying this kind of stunt again?"

"Why not? Next time, we'll get it right. You can't stop us. We're Quality, and you're not—not anymore. What we do is our business and nothing to do with you. You're not one of us anymore, Buchan, and your precious heroics here tonight don't change a thing. You're still nothing more than a dirty little Sister-lover, and we don't want you here."

Fisher stepped briskly forward, punched Brunel out, and took the grimoire from his unconscious body. She looked round at the watching crowd.

"Any objections?"

No one said anything, and most of the Quality looked away to avoid catching her eye. Fisher turned her back on them and handed the grimoire to Buchan.

"You have to know how to talk to these people. Shall we go?"

Buchan and Hightower exchanged a brief smile, and then bowed formally to each other. Buchan left the ballroom through the open double doors, followed by Hawk and

Fisher. Hawk turned back to shut the doors, and came face to face with the silent, staring Quality. He'd helped save their lives, but all he could see in their faces was resentment, and perhaps even hate. They'd been saved by a social inferior who didn't even have the decency to be apologetic about it. Hawk grinned at them, winked, and closed the doors on their disapproving scowls.

Hawk and Fisher and Buchan returned to God Squad headquarters to find Rowan and Tomb sitting slumped and shattered in their usual chairs in the drawing room. Apparently clearing up the mess left on the Street of Gods had been a major undertaking, and was still continuing even now, but they'd done all they could. The Beings remained in their churches and temples, and their followers had retired to lick their wounds and plot more trouble for the future. Everything was quiet for the moment, but it was a false peace, and everyone knew it. They were just waiting for the next dead Being, and then there would be God War on the Street of Gods. And not even the Exorcist Stone would be enough to stop that. Tomb had sent an urgent message to the Council's circle of sorcerers, bringing them up to date on the situation and asking for help and support, but as usual the circle was split by factions and intrigues, and probably wouldn't even respond till it was too late.

"I don't know why I feel so bitter about it," said Tomb tiredly. "This is Haven, after all."

Rowan's mouth twitched in something that might have been meant as a smile. She didn't just look tired, she looked exhausted. Her face was pale and slack, with dark bruises of fatigue under her eyes.

"Are you feeling all right, lady Rowan?" Hawk asked politely.

"I'm fine," said Rowan. "I just need a rest, that's all."

Her voice was flat and strained, and they could all see the effort it took her just to speak. Tomb cleared his throat uncertainly.

"Rowan, I really think we'd all be a lot happier if you'd let us call in a doctor, just to have a look at you. . . . "

"How many more times do I have to tell you?" snapped Rowan. Her anger produced two fiery red spots on her cheeks, but her face remained dull and impassive, as though the facial muscles were simply too tired to respond. "I don't need a doctor, I don't need fussing over, and most of all I don't need you crawling around me all the time. Why won't you all just leave me in peace?"

There was an awkward pause, and then Buchan rose unhurriedly from his chair. "Come on, Tomb. Let's raid the kitchen and see what we can find there. I don't know about you, but I'm starving. It's typical we had to have our busiest day in months on the one day in the week our servants have off."

Tomb nodded without looking at him, and the two men left the drawing room, Buchan pulling the door firmly shut behind them. Hawk and Fisher looked at each other.

"I hate to press you on this, lady Rowan," said Hawk firmly, "but if there is something seriously wrong with you, we need to know about it. Things are going from bad to worse out there on the Street, and we have to know if we can depend on you in a crisis."

Rowan shifted tiredly in her chair. "Yes. I suppose you do. And it would feel so good to talk about it to someone. But you have to swear not to tell Buchan and Tomb. Especially Tomb." She looked at Hawk and Fisher in turn, fixing them with her piercing eyes in her weary face, and waiting until they'd both nodded in agreement. "I have cancer. It's well-established and very advanced, and there's nothing that can be done about it. I thought for a long time I could cure it myself, with my knowledge of potions. By the time I discovered I couldn't, it was too late. It's spread too far for alchemy to do any good now. I've talked to experts. There are spells that might work, but I don't have that kind of money. I've got a month or so left; maybe a little more.

"You mustn't tell Tomb. It would upset him. He hasn't the power to cure me himself, and the dear fool would bankrupt himself trying to raise the money to buy a cure. It's better that he doesn't know."

"But surely . . . one of the Gods could do something," said Fisher uncertainly. "I mean, they do miracles. Don't they?"

"I used to think that," said Rowan. "But if I've learned anything here, it's that there are no Gods on the Street of Gods. I looked really hard, trying to find just one, but all I found were supernatural Beings with no love for the God Squad."

She broke off as the door opened, and Tomb and Buchan came in bearing trays of cold food. For various reasons no one had much to say while they ate, so the meal passed for the most part in silence. Rowan just picked at her food, pushing it back and forth on her plate, and finally she put it to one side and quietly announced she was going back to bed and didn't want to be disturbed. Everyone nodded, and Tomb wished her good night. She left the room without answering, shutting the door firmly behind her. The others finished their food, and sat for a while in silence, thinking their separate thoughts.

"You mustn't mind Rowan," said Tomb finally, to Hawk and Fisher. "It's just her way. She'll be a lot better once she's had a little rest."

"Sure," said Hawk. "We understand."

"Now, if you'll excuse me, I have to be going out again." Tomb pushed his empty plate to one side and stood up.

"Already?" said Fisher. "We only just finished putting down that riot and clearing up after the Hellfire Club. What else is there that needs doing?"

Tomb smiled. "Nothing for you to worry about, Captain. This is just some old personal business that I have to attend to. I won't be long. I'll see you again, later."

He nodded generally to them all, and left. The door was still closing when Buchan got to his feet.

"Afraid I must be off as well. Tomb isn't the only one who's had to neglect his personal life of late. I'll be back in an hour or two. If you have to go out as well, don't

worry about Rowan. There are wards around the house to
keep her safe and alert Tomb if she needs anything. Now
I really must be going."

And as quickly as that, he was gone. Hawk and Fisher
looked at each other. "I'll follow Tomb," said Hawk. "You
follow Buchan. Right?"

"Right," said Fisher. "There are too many secrets around
here for my liking. You know, those have to be two of the
flimsiest excuses I've ever heard."

"I get the feeling they're both under pressure," said Hawk.
"And I don't just mean the trouble on the Street. They probably intended to go out a lot earlier, but got sidetracked by
the riot and the Hellfire Club. Right. They've had enough
time to get a good start by now. Let's go."

They got to their feet and hurried out into the corridor.
Hawk spotted one of Tomb's long hooded robes hanging
on a wall hook, and slipped it on instead of his own distinctive Guard's cloak. With the hood pulled well forward,
he looked like just another priest. He glanced at Fisher.

"Maybe you should try a disguise, too."

Fisher shook her head. "Six-foot muscular blond women
tend to stand out in a crowd, no matter what they're wearing. I'll just have to be careful, that's all. It's dark out, so as
long as I keep well back and stick to the shadows, I should
be all right. I'll meet you two hours from now at the Dead
Dog tavern. Our usual booth. Sound good to you?"

"Great," said Hawk. "Maybe now we'll get a break on
this case, and find a motive that makes sense. The way
things are going, I'd settle for a motive that doesn't make
sense. Now let's move it, before we lose them."

Hawk had no trouble locating Tomb. The sorcerer was
striding down the Street of Gods at a pace that kept threatening to break into a run. People saw the scowl on his face
and got out of his way fast. Hawk strode along after him,
not even trying to be inconspicuous. Even at this late hour
of the evening there were crowds of priests and acolytes
and worshippers bustling back and forth, getting on with

the business of life that the riot had only briefly interrupted. Hawk was just another robed figure among many. Not
that Tomb would have noticed anyway. He shouldered his
way through the crowd with utter indifference to the snarls
and curses this earned him, apparently entirely preoccupied
with wherever he was going. Hawk had been banking on
that. If Tomb even suspected he was being followed, he
would undoubtedly have any number of spells to deal with
the situation, few if any of them pleasant.

Tomb strode on, ignoring the manifestations that haunted
the sidewalks and alleyways. Hawk did his best to do the
same, but was momentarily thrown when an acolyte in a
cheap crimson robe stepped directly in front of him to beg for
a blessing. Hawk put a hand on the acolyte's shaven head,
muttered something about peace and joy and brotherhood,
and hurried after Tomb, hoping fervently that he hadn't
inadvertently invoked a nearby Being by accident. You
had to be careful what you said on the Street of Gods.
You could never be sure who was listening.

He followed Tomb down into the low-rent section of
the Street of Gods, where the twisting back streets and
alleyways turned in upon themselves, offering sanctuary
to Beings and beliefs who had fallen on hard times. A
last harbour for forgotten Gods and fading philosophies.
Hawk hung well back as Tomb approached a nondescript,
weather-beaten door set into a dirty white wall. The sorcerer produced a heavy iron key from a hidden pocket
and unlocked the large iron padlock. The door creaked
open under his hand, and he disappeared inside, pulling
the door shut behind him.

Hawk quickly took up a position in a shadowed doorway
overlooking the street, in case this was only a way stop and
the sorcerer might reappear unexpectedly. Long moments
passed. No one moved in the narrow back street. Hawk
bit his lip, scowling thoughtfully. What the hell was Tomb
doing here? It couldn't be anything illegal; the sorcerer had
made no attempt to disguise his appearance. But what was
so important to Tomb that it could drag him down here at

this time of the night, when he was clearly already exhausted from coping with the riot? Hawk left his hiding place and padded silently over to the shabby door. He listened carefully, but everything seemed quiet within. He tried the door handle and raised an eyebrow as it turned easily under his hand, and the door swung open. Hawk froze as the door hinges creaked softly, but no one came to investigate. He slipped inside and eased the door shut behind him.

The narrow hallway was lit by a single lamp on the wall. Hawk tested the glass with his fingertips. It was barely warm. Tomb must have lit the lamp when he came in, which suggested there was no one here but the sorcerer. The walls were bare wood. They might have been waxed or polished a long time ago, but now there was only a thick coating of dust on the dull surfaces. Whatever this place was, no one had lived in it for a long time. There were no doors leading off the hallway. Hawk followed it to its end, where it turned a sharp corner and became a long narrow stairway leading down into darkness. Hawk scowled at the bottomless gloom, and then reached for the stub of candle and box of matches he kept in his cloak pocket for emergencies. His fingers scrabbled futilely against rough cloth for a long moment before he remembered he was wearing one of Tomb's robes instead of his Guard's cloak. He cursed under his breath, and padded back down the hall to fetch the lamp.

The stairway didn't look nearly so menacing in the lamplight, but even so he still hesitated at the top of the stairs. When all was said and done, following a sorcerer into an unknown situation was never a Good Idea. There could well be a magical bodyguard or booby trap waiting for him at the foot of the stairs. The suppressor stone might protect him . . . but it was still in Fisher's pocket. Hawk shook his head quickly, and drew his axe. He'd faced sorcerers before with nothing but cold steel in his hand, and he was damned if he'd let his nerves get the better of him now.

He descended slowly into the dark, lamp in one hand, axe in the other, ears straining for any sound down below. The walls were bare stone, rough and crumbling and splotched here and there with clumps of lichen. What the hell was Tomb doing in a dump like this? It couldn't be anything commonplace or innocent, or he'd have said where he was going. Since he hadn't, that meant Tomb either wouldn't or couldn't explain. Hawk didn't like secrets. Particularly when they left him in the dark in the middle of a murder enquiry. The stairs ended at a simple wooden door, standing slightly ajar. Light shone round its edges. Hawk stayed put on the bottom step and chewed his bottom lip thoughtfully. He seemed to have spent an awful lot of time hovering outside ominous-looking doors recently, and none of them had led him anywhere pleasant. He hefted his axe, took a deep breath and let it go, and kicked the door open.

"Come in, Captain Hawk," said Tomb. "I've been waiting for you."

The sorcerer was sitting on a plain wooden stool, a few yards beyond the doorway. Above and around him loomed a bare stone cavern, maybe twenty feet high and almost as wide. A pale blue light flickered around the sorcerer, gleaming brightly on metallic traces in the rock. There was no one else there, only the sorcerer Tomb. Hawk stayed put in the doorway, looking around him. There had to be someone else there. Tomb wouldn't have come all this way just to sit in a cave by himself.

"How long have you known I was here?" he asked finally, careful to keep his voice calm and relaxed.

"Quite some time, Captain. I wouldn't be much of a sorcerer if I didn't know when I was being spied on, now would I? Don't worry; I'm not angry. In your position, I'd probably have done the same. Probably. I like the robe, by the way. It suits you."

"Tomb, what are you doing here?"

"It's rather difficult to put into words, Captain. But if you'll stop skulking in the shadows and come and join me, I'll do my best to explain."

Hawk mentally tossed a coin, shrugged, and stepped forward. He might as well, he wasn't learning anything useful where he was. The moment he crossed the threshold, the Presence washed over him like a wave. It filled the cavern; a vast, implacable but utterly intangible Presence. It was like nothing but itself; a living entity with no physical existence, but so real that Hawk could almost feel its heartbeat against his skin. He looked wonderingly at Tomb, who smiled faintly.

"Le Bel Inconnu; the Fair Unknown. It was worshipped as a God long ago, in another place. My family served as its priests for generations. But we are both far from home now, this God and I. It seems I am the last of my line, and when Le Bel Inconnu discovered it was dying, it had no one else to turn to but me."

"Dying?" said Hawk. "How can a God die? It doesn't even have a body!"

"Things are never that simple, Hawk. Especially not here, on the Street of Gods. There is a time for everything, a beginning and an end for all that exists. Le Bel Inconnu was once a great Being, and knew the worship of millions. Now it is almost completely forgotten, nothing more than an obscure footnote in some of the older histories. It has no followers and no priests. It came here to die, Hawk, to fade quietly away into the nothing it came from, and go to whatever afterlife Gods go to. I spend what time with it I can, and never know from one day to the next whether it will still be here the next time I call."

"But why all the secrecy?" said Hawk.

Tomb sighed tiredly. "No member of the Deity Division is allowed to worship a God, Captain Hawk. Religion and faith are not for us. It's the law. How else could the Beings on the Street respect our judgements, and be bound by them, unless they could be sure we showed no favour to any of them? But I can't abandon Le Bel Inconnu. No one should have to go into the dark alone, with no one to care or even know they've gone. But if word of my vigil were to get out, I'd have to leave the God Squad. I don't want that. I've given my life to the Squad. Before I took over, it was a mess. No one took it seriously, least of all the Beings. I changed all that. Made the Squad a power to be reckoned with. The Street of Gods had known almost ten years of peace . . . until the God murders began." He looked unflinchingly at Hawk. "Are you going to report this, Captain Hawk?"

Hawk looked about him, feeling the Presence beat on the air like the fluttering wings of a dying bird. He shook his head slowly. "There's nothing to tell, Tomb. Nothing to do with the case I'm working on. I'll see you later."

He turned away from the sorcerer and his God, and made his way back through the darkness to the life and bustle of the Street of Gods.

Fisher followed Buchan through the crowded Street, elbowing aside people who momentarily blocked her view of the man she was following. No one objected out loud. Even on the Street of Gods, people knew about Captain Fisher. She was careful to stay well back, but Buchan showed no signs of caring if he was being followed. The man was deathly tired; Fisher could see it in the way he walked, the way he held his head too carefully erect. But even so, nobody bothered him. They knew about Buchan's reputation, too.

Buchan, with Fisher still a discreet distance behind him, made his way along the Street, passing through the usual crowd of priests and worshippers. Riot or no riot, business went on as usual on the Street of Gods. From time to time people called out greetings to Buchan, some clearly false and some as clearly not, but he answered them all with the same preoccupied nod and wave of the hand. A few people looked as though they might call out to Fisher, but she glared at them until they changed their minds.

After a while, she began to realise Buchan was heading into the high-rent section of the Street of Gods. The churches and temples became richer and more ornate, works of art in their own right, and there was a much better class of worshippers, most of whom seemed scandalized at Fisher's presence in their midst. Fisher glared at them all impartially. Buchan finally stopped outside one of the more modest buildings. It was three storeys high, with rococo carvings and elegant wrought iron. The building had an anonymous air to it, as though it was a place for those who were just passing through, not staying. The kind of temporary residence popular among people on the way up or on the way down. The management didn't care which, as long as it got cash in advance.

Buchan produced a key and unlocked the front door. He stepped inside, and shut the door firmly behind him. Fisher scowled. What was Buchan doing in a place like this? She hesitated a moment, not sure what to do next. Hawk was the one who usually tailed people. She couldn't just barge in and start asking questions about Buchan. He wasn't supposed to know he was being followed. She frowned. She couldn't just hang about outside the place, either. People would notice. She made her way round the side of the building and down a narrow alleyway she hoped would lead to a back entrance. Maybe she could sneak in that way and find some low-level staff she could intimidate into providing some answers. Fisher always preferred the direct approach.

She hurried down the alleyway, keeping to the shadows when she remembered, rounded the corner, and sighed with relief as she took in the back of the building. It didn't look nearly as impressive as the front, with uneven paintwork and a filthy back yard. Judging by the smell, the drains weren't working too well either. There was one back door, strictly functional and clearly a servants' and tradesman's entrance. Fisher started toward it, only to stop dead as the door suddenly swung open. She darted behind a pile of stacked crates, crouched down, and watched with interest as a hunched and furtive figure pushed the door shut. He was wearing a torn and ratty-looking cloak with the hood pulled forward, but from her angle Fisher could see the face clearly. It was Buchan. He reached up to pull the hood even further forward, looked quickly around him, and then hurried along the alley and out onto the Street.

Fisher grinned broadly, and stayed where she was a moment to give him a good start. Buchan was definitely up to something. Where could he be going, that he couldn't afford to be recognised? Buchan was known and welcomed pretty much everywhere outside of High Society. She slipped out from behind the crates, ran silently down the alley, and emerged on the Street just in time to see him walking unhurriedly away. He was so confident in his disguise he didn't even bother to look behind him. Fisher stayed well back anyway, just in case. She was beginning to get the hang of following people.

Buchan led her through the luxurious high-rent district of the Street of Gods, where the magnificent buildings struggled to outdo each other in splendour and ostentatious opulence. He passed them all by without looking, until he came to the largest and most ornate structure yet. It was as broad as any three churches, and an amazing four storeys high. Fisher didn't even want to think how much money the owners must be paying for spells to protect the place from the violent spring gales. Massive bay windows jutted out onto the Street, and there was gold and silver scrollwork in abundance. And enough intricately carved stonework to have kept entire families of stonemasons busy for generations. There was one door, centrally placed: a huge slab of polished oak, bearing a large brass knocker. Engraved into the stone above the door was a single ornate symbol, known and reviled throughout the Low Kingdoms. Buchan knocked twice, and waited. Even from across the Street, Fisher could feel his impatience. The door opened, and Buchan quickly disappeared inside. Fisher bit her lower lip thoughtfully as the door swung shut behind him. In a way, she was almost disappointed. You didn't expect a man like the legendary Charles Buchan to go sneaking off to the notorious Sisters of Joy.

Fisher didn't approve of the Sisters. They were dangerous. Like a rose with poisoned thorns. In her time as a Guard, Fisher had seen men entrapped by the Sisters and betrayed by their own weaknesses. They lost all strength and dignity, giving up on everything except the object of their obsession. They threw away their jobs, alienated their families, and sold everything they could lay their hands on to make donations to the Sisters. By the time the Sister concerned had sucked them dry, it must almost have come as a relief.

Fisher folded her arms and leaned back against a church wall, staring thoughtfully at the house of the Sisters of Joy. What the hell was Buchan doing here? It wasn't at all in character for the great romantic she'd heard so much about. Of course, she if anyone had good reason to know that people weren't always what their storied personas made them out to be. But still . . . What if there was something else going on here? Something . . . deeper. Fisher pushed herself away from the wall and unfolded her arms. Whatever Buchan was mixed up in, she wanted to know about it. There were too many secrets in this case. She checked her sword moved freely in its scabbard, marched over to the Sisters' door, and knocked loudly. There was a long pause. Passersby looked at Fisher in various ways. Fisher glared at them all impartially.

The door finally opened a few inches. Fisher put her shoulder to the door and shoved it all the way open. She stalked in past the astonished Sister she'd sent flying backwards, and looked around her. There was an understated elegance to the hallway, with delicately fashioned furniture and a deep pile carpet. An ornate glass-and-crystal chandelier hung from the ceiling, and the air was scented with rose petals. It was actually quite impressive in a quiet way. Fisher had been in country mansions that looked less refined. Until you took in the obscene murals on the walls. Fisher had never seen anything like them. She felt a blush rising to her cheeks, and looked quickly away. The Sister had recovered her composure, and took the opportunity to bow respectfully to Fisher. She was very lovely, in an open, healthy way that owed nothing to makeup, with curly russet hair and a heart-shaped face. Her long flowing gown was spotlessly white and hugged her magnificent figure in all the right places. She couldn't have been more than nineteen or twenty. Fisher felt decidedly battered and dowdy in comparison, which didn't do a thing for her temper.

The Sister bowed again, showing off her cleavage, and smiled widely at Fisher. "Welcome to the house of pleasure and contentment, Captain. In what way may we be of service to you?"

"I'm looking for Buchan," said Fisher flatly. "Where is he?"

The Sister shook her head, still smiling. "We guarantee complete anonymity to all who come here, Captain. Within this house our patrons are free to adopt whatever names or characters they wish. We ask no questions, demand no answers. We offer comfort and security to all who come here, and we protect their privacy. Whatever your business is with the man you seek, it will have to wait until he has left these walls."

Fisher scowled. She knew a set speech when she heard one. "All right, we'll do it the hard way." She reached out, took a handful of the Sister's gown, and pulled her close so that their faces were only inches apart. "I'm Captain Fisher of the city Guard. I'm here on official business, and I want to see Charles Buchan right now. And if you or anyone else gets in my way, I am going to bounce them off the nearest wall till their ears bleed. Got it?"

The Sister never flinched once. She met Fisher's gaze calmly, and when she spoke, her voice was mild and even and unafraid. "Kill me, if you wish. My Sisters will avenge me. The secrets of this house are not mine to tell, and I will die rather than divulge them. No Sister here will tell you anything, Captain. We will not betray those who trust us."

Fisher swore briefly, and let the Sister go. She felt obscurely ashamed, as though she'd been caught bullying a child. She had no doubt the Sister meant what she said. Her voice and face held the unquestioning certainty of the fanatic. Probably brainwashed. Or under a geas' compulsion. Or both. She sighed, and stepped away from the Sister. When in doubt, be direct.

"Buchan!" she roared at the top of her voice. "Charles Buchan! I know you're here. Either get the hell down here and talk to me or I'll go out into the Street and tell everyone I see that you're in here. What do you think would happen to your reputation as a member of the God Squad if word got out that you were a Sister-lover? Buchan! Talk to me!"

There was a long pause, and then a second Sister appeared from a concealed doorway. She wore the same white gown and was equally lovely, in a cool aristocratic way, but she was nearer Fisher's age, and though she smiled and bowed respectfully, her eyes were cold and hard. "There's no need for threats, Captain. The person you seek has agreed to see you. Even though he was assured he didn't have to. And Captain; if he hadn't agreed, you would not have got any further in this house. We have spells to ensure our privacy. Very unpleasant spells. Now, if you'll come with me, please . . ."

Fisher gave the Sister one of her best scowls, just to make it clear who was really in charge here, and then followed her through a series of stairs and corridors to a plain anonymous door on the second floor. The Sister bowed deeply and left her there. Fisher knocked once, and walked straight in without waiting for an answer. The room was luxurious without being overbearing, and the furnishings had the understated elegance of old money. Fisher wondered fleetingly just how old the Sisters' establishment was, and then fixed her attention on Charles Buchan. He was standing stiffly beside a chair on which sat a beautiful young woman, a pale willowy blonde barely into her twenties. *Is that it?* thought Fisher. *All this secrecy, just because he's fallen for a girl young enough to be his daughter?* And yet . . . there was something wrong with the scene. She turned and pushed the door shut, to give herself a moment to think. Buchan's attitude; that was what was wrong. As soon as she turned back, she recognised what it was. Buchan didn't look ashamed, or indignant, or obsessed with the girl; he looked protective toward her, as though all that mattered was protecting the Sister from Fisher. If he cared at all about being found out, he was doing an excellent job of hiding it. He met Fisher's gaze unwaveringly.

"Captain Fisher. I should have known you'd find us out, if anyone would."

Fisher shrugged. "I don't like secrets. I take it personally when people hide things from me. Particularly when it affects a case we're supposed to be working on together."

"There's no connection between this and the God murders, Captain. You have my word on that. Annette, I'd like you to meet Captain Fisher, one of my colleagues on the God Squad. Captain, this is Annette. My daughter."

Annette smiled at Fisher, who just stood there, completely thrown.

"Why don't we all sit down?" Buchan suggested. "This is going to take some explaining."

"Yes," said Fisher. "I think it is."

Buchan pulled up a chair beside Annette, and Fisher sat on a chair facing them. Buchan took a deep breath and plunged straight in.

"Annette's mother was a young Lady from a rival Family. The heads of our Families weren't talking to each other, and there had even been a few duels. Nothing unusual, but it was all very tense, and the worst possible time for us to meet and fall in love. But we were young and foolish, and nothing mattered to us except each other. We were going to run away and be married secretly. We even had some naive hopes that our marriage would bring the Families back together again.

"But she became pregnant. Her Family found out, and when she wouldn't name the father, they sent her out of the city to stay with relatives until it was all over. She died giving birth to Annette. Her Family let everyone assume the child was dead, too. They weren't interested in raising some bastard half-breed mongrel, so they gave her to the city orphanage.

"I went a little crazy after I heard my love was dead. I'd do anything, for a laugh or a thrill or just to fill my time. I chased women endlessly, trying to find someone who could replace the one I'd lost. Finally it all got out of hand, and I ended up on the God Squad. It was interesting work, and it passed the time. And then I came here, on business for the Squad, and found Annette. She looked just like her mother. I investigated her background, and worked out who she was. I thought about it for a long time, and then came here and introduced myself.

"She's very precious to me. For all my affairs, Annette is my only child. We sit and talk for hours.

"But somehow word of my visits to this house got out, at least in High Society, and I couldn't explain why I came here. Someday Annette may choose to leave this place and take her rightful place in High Society. The Quality must never know of her time here. They can be very old-fashioned about some things. So, I decided to let people think what they liked about my visits to the Sisters of Joy. My friends and family disowned me, and the Quality turned their back on me. But Annette's secret was safe. The rest you know."

Fisher shook her head slowly. "That is so crazy a story it has to be true."

"Will you keep our secret?" said Buchan. "For her sake, if not for mine."

"Sure," said Fisher. "Why not? Hawk will have to know, but I don't see any reason why it should go any further." She looked at Annette. "Are you happy here, lass? Really happy? If they've got any kind of hold over you, I can take care of it. No one's stupid enough to upset me and Hawk. If you want to leave, just say the word. I'll escort you out of here right now."

Annette smiled and shook her head. "Thank you, Captain, but I'm quite happy here. As I keep telling my father, I wasn't brainwashed into joining the Sisters of Joy, there isn't any geas keeping me here, and if I want to leave I'm perfectly free to do so at any time. The Sisterhood is a vocation, and one I believe in. How many other religions do you know that are simply dedicated to making people happy? Perhaps someday, I'll feel differently, but even then I don't think I'll be joining High Society. From what I've heard of the Quality, I doubt we'd get on. In the meantime, my father and I have each other. No one ever told me who my father was. I never dreamed it would turn out to be the legendary Charles Buchan."

Buchan stirred uncomfortably. "You don't want to pay too much attention to those stories, Annette."

"Why? Aren't they true?"

"Well, yes. Most of them. But I'm a reformed character, now I've found you."

Annette raised an eyebrow. "Reformed? You?"

Buchan grinned. "Partly reformed."

Father and daughter laughed quietly together. Fisher got to her feet, feeling decidedly superfluous, and wished them both goodbye. They favoured her with a quick smile and a wave. Fisher smiled quickly in return and left them to each other.

The Dead Dog Tavern was a seedy little dive in the Northside, not that far from the Street of Gods. The air was full of smoke, the sawdust on the floor hadn't been changed in weeks, and the only reason the drinks weren't watered was that the patrons would have lynched the innkeeper if he'd tried it. Hawk and Fisher had used the Dead Dog as a meeting place before. It was the kind of place where everyone minded his own business, and expected everyone else to do likewise. Or else. Having Hawk and Fisher around didn't keep people away; the other patrons just kept their voices down and one eye always on the nearest exit. Hawk and Fisher liked the Dead Dog because it was quiet and convenient and nobody bothered them. There weren't many places like that in the Northside.

Hawk glared into his ale, gave a frustrated sigh, and slouched down in his chair. "Dammit, we're getting nowhere with this case, Isobel. No matter which way we turn, we end up going round and round in bloody circles."

Fisher took a healthy drink from her mug, and shook her head. "Don't give up now, Hawk. We're getting close; I can feel it. Look; we know how the God murders took place. Somebody used the Exorcist Stone. That tells us who; it has to be one of the God Squad. Did you notice that when we talked about Bode's death, and the lack of magic at his house, none of them even mentioned the Exorcist Stone as a possible murder weapon? Significant, that. All we have to do is find a way to narrow it down from three suspects to one."

"It's not that simple, Isobel, and you know it. First, the Council put a geas on all of them, specifically to prevent them misusing the Stone. If the compulsion spell had some-how been broken, the Council would have known immedi-ately. And second, we still don't have a motive for the murders. What do any of them have to gain by killing Gods?"

They sat in silence for a while, nursing their ale.

"Let's go over everybody again, one at a time," said Hawk. "The one thing the three of them have in common is that they all have secrets. Buchan has a daughter who's a Sister of Joy. Tomb has broken God Squad rules by wor-shipping Le Bel Inconnu. And Rowan is dying of cancer and doesn't want the others to know about it. Secrets often make for good motives. People will do desperate things to keep a secret hidden.

"So, suppose the dead Gods knew about Buchan's daugh-ter. Priests do talk to each other, even when they're sup-posed to be enemies. They're in the same line of business, after all. Word could have got around. What if the murdered Gods had tried to use that knowledge, to put pressure on Buchan to look the other way on occasion? It could be a very handy thing for a Being to have a member of the God Squad in his pocket."

"It's a nice idea," said Fisher. "But I don't think it's Buchan. In order to come and go without being seen by the Gods' followers, the killer must have had access to some kind of sorcery, and Buchan doesn't have any. He had to use an ordinary disguise when he went to visit his daughter, remember? And besides, if he'd had any magic, he'd have used it against that creature at the Hellfire Club, wouldn't he?"

"Not necessarily," said Hawk. "He could be trying to put us off the scent by not using magic when we're around. He might have known you were following him."

Fisher sniffed. "Firstly, if he'd known I was following him, he wouldn't have led me to the Sisters and revealed his secret. Secondly, I don't really think Buchan's that clever, to be honest. He's famed for many things, but subtlety's not one of them. I think we'd be better off taking a hard look at Tomb. Now, he has a motive that makes sense. If the Council knew about his private God, they'd throw him off the Squad, and Tomb's put a lot of time and effort into making the God Squad a force to be reckoned with. He might see a threat to himself as a threat to the Squad, and act accordingly. So, if another Being had found out, and threatened to tell on him . . . Hey, wait a minute, I've just had another thought. What if the God killings were some kind of sacrifice to Tomb's God? To make it stronger, more powerful?"

"Could be," said Hawk, thinking about it. "Certainly Tomb's got enough sorcery to get in and out of the churches undetected."

"And he certainly knew his way around when he showed us the murder sites earlier on."

"No. We can't single him out on that. According to the informer Lacey, all of the God Squad had visited the dead Beings previously."

"All right," said Fisher. "Forget that. But the rest fits."

"It still doesn't explain how he broke the geas without the Council circle of sorcerers knowing. That's supposed to be impossible."

Fisher nodded reluctantly. "All right. Let's leave Tomb for a moment and look at Rowan. She's got enough sorcery to move unseen, and she's certainly got no love for the Gods."

"Sure," said Hawk. "But what's her motive?"

"Revenge," said Fisher. "She's dying, and she wants to kill as many of the Gods she despises as she can before she dies."

"That's pushing it a bit, isn't it?"

Fisher shrugged. The two of them drank more ale, their scowls deepening as they struggled with the problem. People around them took in the danger signs, quietly finished their drinks, and made for the exits.

"I don't know," said Hawk. "Whatever motives the God Squad have, I keep coming back to the geas. Either one of them's found a way round the compulsion spell, which is supposed to be impossible, or it has to be somebody else. Maybe it's really the sorcerer Bode after all, using the Dark Men as weapons. Remember, two of the Gods had been torn apart, which would seem to indicate that the killer had great physical strength."

"You may have something there," said Fisher slowly. "But have you ever noticed that the Dark Men never attack us except when the God Squad aren't around?"

They looked at each other for a moment. "Are you suggesting one of the God Squad is the controlling mind behind the Dark Men?" said Hawk finally.

"Why not? It fits!" Fisher leaned forward excitedly. "that's how someone on the Squad could use the Exorcist Stone! The geas was placed on a specific person, once that person was in another body—a Dark Man homunculus—he or she became a different individual, free to use the Exorcist Stone without any restraints!"

"You're right," said Hawk. "It does fit. I think we're finally getting somewhere. And it means we can rule out Buchan as the murderer. He was there when the Dark Man attacked us at the Hellfire Club. And anyway, he doesn't have the sorcery needed to transfer his mind from one body to another. You know, more and more makes sense now. Let's assume our God Squad murderer is the same person who hired Bode. That's why Bode sometimes didn't recognise his friends on the Street of Gods: Someone else was using a duplicate of Bode's body at the

time! Bode's body could ask questions that a member of
the God Squad couldn't ask without appearing suspicious.
Whoever gave Bode his mission wasn't just hiring Bode
as a person, they were also hiring his body! Hell's teeth,
that's devious."

"Don't get too excited," said Fisher dryly. "We still
haven't got a motive. Let's try it from a different angle.
What was Bode, or the person inside Bode's body, looking
for on the Street of Gods?"

"Ways of getting to the Beings?"

"No, they already knew how to do that as part of the
God Squad." Fisher scowled, and doodled aimlessly in the
spilt ale on the table. "Bode, or whoever was inside his double, was asking questions about the Gods themselves. Their
histories, their powers, their natures. It was the answers to
these questions that marked the Beings for death."

"But what's so important about those questions?" said
Hawk. "Every tourist on the Street asks questions like
those."

"And they end up with tourist answers. But a sorcerer
and a member of the God Squad might just get an answer
that meant something. . . . " Fisher sat up straight suddenly. "Hawk, I think I've got it! Remember the Being who
was stabbed to death—the Sundered Man? That priestess of
his, Sister Anna, was really bitter about his death because
it meant she'd wasted her life worshipping something that
wasn't really a God after all! I don't know about the last
death, the Lord of the New Flesh, but both the other dead
Beings died when the Exorcist Stone removed all the magic from their vicinity. The Dread Lord fell apart, and the
Carmadine Stalker aged to death. That's what Bode and
his employer were looking for on the Street of Gods: proof
that a Being wasn't a God after all but just a supernatural
creature with magic powers and a following."

"Not quite," said Hawk suddenly. "Turn it around. They
weren't looking for Beings among the Gods; they were trying to find one real God among the Beings, and killing the
ones who failed the test."

"But why would Tomb or Rowan be so desperate to find a real God?" Fisher's eyes widened suddenly. "Because one of them needed a miracle cure! It's Rowan; it has to be! It all fits together. The killings only started after she joined the Squad. She went to Bode when her potions couldn't control the cancer, probably hoping he'd have something that would help her. After all, he was an alchemist as well as a sorcerer. He didn't have a cure, but he did have the Dark Men. Which was just what she needed to investigate the Beings. She must have been getting pretty desperate by then. She couldn't ask questions on the street herself, so she got Bode to do it for her, and sometimes did it herself in one of the homunculus bodies. Every time she thought she'd found a real God, she'd go to them and beg for a miracle cure. If they couldn't or wouldn't help her, she destroyed them, using the Exorcist Stone and the strength of the Dark Man. Presumably out of revenge for wasting her limited time."

"No wonder she's spent so much time in bed recently," said Hawk. "Her mind was out and about, attacking us in a Dark Man body. But why did she kill Bode?"

Fisher shrugged. "Maybe he found out about the God killings, and wanted to call it off. She couldn't allow that. She killed him the same way she killed the Beings. She must really have panicked when she found out the same two Guards who investigated Bode's murder had been seconded to the God Squad. That's why she tried to get rid of us when we first arrived. And why she kept attacking us through the Dark Men. We were so close to the answer all along, and didn't know it. . . . But then, why did she tell us she had cancer?"

"Trying for sympathy, I expect," said Hawk. "Hoping that would distract us from seeing her as the killer. It almost worked. You don't expect a dying woman to be a murderer. We've got to get back to the Squad and confront her."

"What's the hurry? She's not going anywhere in her weakened condition."

"Oh no? What's to stop her leaving her dying body behind and living on in a healthy Dark Man body?"

"A woman living in a man's body?" Fisher wrinkled her nose. "That's kinky."

"Don't knock it till you've tried it. Now let's go. I wouldn't put it past Rowan to have a few more tricks up her sleeve. And we can't afford another dead God."

7

Return of the Dark Man

The Street of Gods was unusually quiet. The riot had cleared the air somewhat, and most people were licking their wounds and waiting to see what would happen next. Guards and sorcerers walked the length of the Street, keeping the peace, backed by armored contingents from the Brotherhood of Steel. But in the side streets and back alleys, the dark and shadowed places of the Street of Gods, plots were hatched and plans were whispered. The God War drew steadily nearer, awaiting only one last deadly spark. Anticipation filled the air like the smell of spilt blood, feared and desired in equal measure, as man and God looked each to his own position and saw how it could be worse or better. Change had come to the Street of Gods, and whatever happened, nothing would ever be the same again. Four Beings had been proved to be merely mortal, and no God could feel entirely secure after that.

Hawk and Fisher trudged wearily back to God Squad headquarters, following the shortest route the Street allowed. Hawk yawned continuously, too tired even to raise a hand to cover his mouth. Given the Street of Gods' eccentric attitude to the passing of time, he'd long ago lost track of what hour of which day it was, but it had been a hell of a long time since he'd last had any sleep. His feet were like lead, his legs ached, and

his back was killing him. *Getting old, Hawk.* He smiled
sourly. He always got gloomy when he was tired. Still,
the sooner he and Fisher wrapped up this case, the better.
The more tired you got, the more likely you were to make
mistakes. And making mistakes on a case like this could
get you killed.

The few people still out on the Street gave Hawk and
Fisher plenty of room. Word of their victory over the rogue
Being had spread, and priests and worshippers alike kept
to their best behavior while the two Guards were around.
Even the street preachers lowered the volume a little as they
passed.

God Squad headquarters finally loomed up ahead, and
Hawk allowed himself to relax a little. The small nondescript building, with its old-fashioned lamp shining brightly
over the door, looked actually cosy. Almost there, almost
over. All they had to do was face Rowan with what they
knew, and she'd crack. They always did, when you had
them dead to rights. Some villains even seemed relieved as
you took them off to gaol, as though they were as tired of
the chase as you were. And anyway, Rowan shouldn't be
too difficult to handle. When all was said and done, without
the Exorcist Stone in her hands she was nothing more than
a minor league magic-user with a side line in potions. With
the suppressor stone to protect them from her magic, they
should be safe enough. As long as they didn't drink anything she offered them. A sudden thought struck Hawk, and
he stopped dead in his tracks, his mind working furiously.
Fisher stopped too, and looked at him.

"Hawk? What's the matter?"

"I just thought of something. We've been assuming
Rowan transferred her mind into a Dark Man, then used
the Exorcist Stone against the Beings. Right?"

"Right."

"But if the Exorcist Stone banished all the magic from the
area, it should also have affected the homunculus Rowan
was inhabiting. After all, that's how we beat the original
Dark Man, remember? You fired up the suppressor stone,

and he went out like a light. So if Rowan had used the Exorcist Stone, it would have knocked out the Dark Man she was using and thrown her back into her own body. Which means our whole theory has just gone up in smoke!"

"Don't panic," said Fisher. "The Stone doesn't work that way. It isn't designed to affect *everything* in the area, or it would end up affecting itself, destroying its own power. It has built-in safety guards, like our suppressor stones, so that they don't affect themselves or the people using them. It's only common sense, after all. If you'd paid attention at the morning briefing when the suppressor stones were handed out, you'd have known that."

"Sorry," said Hawk. "You know I'm never any good with technical stuff."

"And you have the nerve to complain because I won't let you carry the suppressor stone. . . . "

"All right. No need to rub it in. Anything else I ought to remember about the stone?"

"Yes . . . " said Fisher slowly. "Unlike the Exorcist Stone, our stones have only a limited amount of magic, and we've been using our stone a hell of a lot just recently. And before you ask: No, there's no telling how badly we've drained it, or how much magic there is left in the stone. These things are prototypes, remember?"

"Great," said Hawk. "Just great." They looked at each other. "If we try and arrest Rowan, and the stone doesn't work, we're going to be in real trouble. Without the stone's magic to counteract hers, she'll just transfer her mind into a Dark Man body and disappear."

"Then we'll just have to hope there is enough magic left in the stone to hold her," said Fisher.

Hawk looked at her. "This case just gets better and better." He thought hard for a moment. "Look. How about if we get one of the others to use the Exorcist Stone? That should prevent her leaving her body."

Fisher nodded. "All right. Who do we ask?"

"Buchan. We can't trust Tomb. He's too close to Rowan."

They continued on their way, frowning thoughtfully. Passersby gave them even more room than usual. The two Guards finally reached God Squad headquarters, and Hawk hammered on the door with his fist. Not the politest way to knock, but Hawk wasn't in a polite mood. There was a long pause, and then Buchan opened the door, sword in hand. He relaxed a little as he saw who it was, sheathed his sword, and nodded politely to them.

"I was wondering what had happened to you two. Officially, we're still on emergency status, but things seem to have calmed down a lot now. The Street's quiet, and the Guard and the Brotherhood of Steel are out in force to make sure it stays that way."

"I'll drink to that," said Hawk. "Is everyone here?"

"Sure. Tomb and Rowan are talking upstairs. Want me to give them a call?"

"Not just yet," said Hawk. "I think the three of us ought to have a word first. In the drawing room. It'll be more private."

Buchan looked at him, and then at Fisher, his face cold but composed. He nodded stiffly, and led the way into the drawing room. Fisher closed the door behind them, and put her back against it so they wouldn't be interrupted before they were finished. Besides, she didn't want Buchan to have the option of leaving. He wasn't going to like what they had to tell him. Fisher couldn't blame him. It always comes hard to find someone you've trusted and fought beside is a traitor. Buchan looked at the two Guards evenly, his gaze firm and unyielding.

"This is about Annette, isn't it?"

"No," said Hawk. "Your secret's safe with us. It's irrelevant to our investigation. We need to talk to you, sir Buchan. We know who the God killer is."

"You do? Who is it?" Buchan looked eagerly from Hawk to Fisher and back again. "Do you need my help with the arrest? Is that it?"

"In a way," said Fisher. "You'd better brace yourself,

Buchan. You're not going to like this."

Buchan frowned uncertainly. "What's going on here?"

"It's Rowan," said Hawk. "She's the God killer. She killed all four Beings, and the sorcerer Bode, too. Probably because he wouldn't go along with her plans."

For a moment, Buchan's face was absolutely slack and empty. Then he shook his head in a dismissive gesture and laughed shakily. "You're crazy. You're out of your minds, both of you. It can't be her! She's one of us. Part of the God Squad. Has been for years. Besides, she's been ill; it couldn't be her."

"It's her," said Hawk. "But she's not going to surrender herself easily. There might be trouble. We could use your help."

"Do you have proof? Hard evidence?"

"Some," said Hawk. "Enough. Now, will you help us?"

"I don't really have a choice, do I?" said Buchan. "If I don't, you'll tell everyone about me and Annette. Right?"

"No," said Fisher. "We don't work that way. Your secret's safe, whatever you decide. But we really could use some backup on this."

"You were right," said Buchan. "I don't like this. What do you want me to do?"

"First," said Hawk, "go up and tell Rowan and Tomb we're back and want to talk to them. If they ask what about, you don't know. Wait till they're safely downstairs, and then while we're having our little chat, you get hold of the Exorcist Stone and activate it. Hopefully our suppressor stone will be enough to hold her, but I'll feel better knowing you're there."

"There's not to be any rough stuff," said Buchan. "I won't stand for any rough stuff. Rowan's done a lot of good work with the Squad, in her time. She even saved my life once. She deserves better than this."

"She brought it on herself," said Fisher. "How many Guards died out there in the riot tonight, do you suppose? The riot she helped bring about?"

"That's enough, Isobel," said Hawk. "He knows."

Buchan turned and headed for the door. He opened it and stepped out into the hallway, then stopped and looked back at Hawk and Fisher. "You'd better be right about this. If you're not, if you're only guessing . . . I'll break you. Rowan is God Squad. We look after our own."

He shut the door firmly behind him, just short of a slam. Hawk and Fisher looked at each other, and then moved as one to the drinks cabinet. They both felt very much in need of a stiff drink, or two.

"He means it, you know," said Fisher.

"Damn right he means it," said Hawk. "This could easily turn very nasty, lass. It wasn't until Buchan asked about proof and evidence that I realised how thin our case actually is. We can show motive and opportunity, and demonstrate how it *could* have been done, but we'd be hard pressed to prove any of it in Court."

"It's a bit late for second thoughts," said Fisher. "We can't put this off; we have to confront her now. All it needs is one more dead Being and all hell will break loose on the Street of Gods. Probably quite literally. We'll just have to face Rowan with what we know, and hope she'll break down and confess."

"And if she doesn't? If she laughs in our faces, and tells us we're crazy?"

"Then I'll swear blind it was all your idea, and nothing to do with me."

"Gosh, thanks," said Hawk. "What would I do without you?"

Rowan and Tomb faced each other across Rowan's bedroom. Rowan was in a towering rage, her face dangerously flushed, but Tomb stood his ground.

"You did *what*, Tomb?"

"I ran a scanning spell on you," said Tomb. "A full body scan. I was worried about you. It seems I had every right to be. You're ill, Rowan, very ill. You have been for some time. Your body's riddled with cancers. I'm amazed you're still able to function as well as you do. I can only assume your potions are effective painkillers, if nothing else." His voice broke, and his pose broke with it. He looked miserably at her, almost pleading. "Why didn't you tell me, Rowan? Did you think you couldn't trust me?"

"I didn't tell you," said Rowan coldly, "because I wanted to avoid a scene like this. How many times do I have to say it, Tomb? This is none of your business. I'm none of your business. I have no interest in your feelings, and your interest in me is annoying when it isn't intrusive. I want you to stay away from me. Dammit, Tomb, get the hell out of my life and leave me alone!"

"I can't. You're dying, Rowan. You must know that. Your condition is so advanced now there's nothing sorcery can do for you anymore. Healers aren't miracle workers. Why didn't you tell me earlier? I could have helped you. . . . "

"I don't want your help! I don't need your help!"

"At least let me tell Buchan. We can handle the God Squad work between us for a while. You have to rest, take things easy. We'll look after you."

"You'd love that, wouldn't you? You do so love to fuss over me. Well, I haven't time for that nonsense anymore. I have things to do, and not much time to do them in."

Tomb looked at her blankly. "Things? What things? What can be more important than this? We're talking about your life, Rowan! If you rest and take things easy, you could have months ahead of you yet. There are still some things I can do, some things I can try. If you don't rest, you'll be dead in a few weeks."

Rowan looked away from him. "A few weeks," she said quietly. "I didn't realise it had got that close. Are you sure?"

"Yes. I'm sorry, Rowan. My scan was very thorough, and there's no room for doubt. Please. Let me help you."

"No." Rowan lifted her head and faced him squarely, perfectly composed. "I've chosen my way and I'll stick to it."

"And if you're wrong?"

"Then I'm wrong!" Rowan smiled suddenly. "Trust me, Tomb. Whatever happens, I'm not going to die."

"Rowan, you have to face this. You can't just turn your back on it. . . . "

"Oh, shut up! Get out of here, Tomb. Find something else to do instead of pestering me. I have some thinking to do."

There was a knock on the door, polite but firm. Rowan strode past Tomb without looking at him, opened the door, and glared at Buchan. "What do you want?"

"Hawk and Fisher are back. They're waiting in the drawing room. They want to talk to us immediately. Apparently they've made a breakthrough on the God murders."

"What kind of breakthrough?" asked Rowan.

"They didn't give me any details. But they seemed quite excited."

"This had better be important," Rowan said, sweeping past him. "I have things to do."

Tomb and Buchan followed her out of the room, each lost in his own separate thoughts.

Rowan stormed into the drawing room and threw herself into her favourite chair. Hawk and Fisher stood together, their faces professionally calm, their hands resting on their sword belts. Rowan studied them both.

"Buchan said something about a breakthrough. What have you found out?"

"The truth," said Hawk. "It took us a while, but we finally got there. We know who the God murderer is."

Tomb entered the room just in time to hear that, and brightened up a little. "Well, that is good news, Captain. When can we expect an arrest?"

"I think you'd better sit down, sir Tomb," said Fisher. "Our News isn't exactly pleasant."

Tomb's smile faded away. He made no move to sit down, and studied their faces closely. "What is this? I don't understand."

"Rowan does," said Hawk. "Don't you, Rowan?"

The mystic met his gaze unflinchingly. "I don't know what you're talking about, Captain."

"All right," said Hawk. "We'll do it the hard way. Rowan, you're under arrest for the murder of four Beings, and the sorcerer Bode. You will come with us to Guard headquarters, where arrangements will be made for your trial. If you wish to make a confession, pen and paper will be provided."

Hawk glanced at Tomb. The sorcerer was staring at him blankly. Rowan hadn't reacted at all, except for a small smile tugging at the corner of her mouth.

"You must really be desperate, if you're reduced to making blind allegations like that," she said calmly. "What proof do you have? Where's your evidence? I have a right to know why I'm being charged."

"There'll be time for that later," said Fisher.

"We'll talk about it now!" snapped Rowan. "I'm a member of the God Squad, in good standing. We have friends in high places. They won't stand by and let you lay all the blame on me, just because you're getting nowhere and the pressure's on you to make an arrest."

"That's right," said Tomb quickly. "I think this has gone quite far enough. You must be mad, both of you. How could it be Rowan? She's been very ill, and was actually confined to her bed when the killings took place! I understand the pressure you must both be under, but I'm damned if I'll let you get away with this. . . . "

"That's enough!" Hawk's voice cut sharply across the sorcerer's bluster. "That's enough, sir Tomb. We have a job to do, and you're not making this any easier for anyone. We know how the murders were committed, and we know why. And if you weren't so blinded by your feelings for Rowan, you'd have probably worked it out for yourself long ago. Rowan, it's time to go. Is there anything you want to take with you, or anything you want to say?"

"I don't think so," said Rowan.

"You're not taking her anywhere!" said Tomb. "I told you; she's ill. She's in no condition to be locked up in some filthy cell. I won't allow it. If she has to be kept somewhere, until she can be proved innocent, she can stay here, under house arrest."

"I'm afraid we can't allow that," said Fisher. "We have to follow procedure."

"This is all irrelevant anyway," said Rowan. "None of you have the power to hold me anywhere."

"Rowan, dear, let me handle this," said Tomb quickly.

"Oh, shut up, Tomb."

Tomb gaped at her as she rose unhurriedly to her feet and smiled defiantly at Hawk and Fisher. Something in the room's atmosphere changed in that moment, and they could all feel it. Without drawing a weapon or moving a muscle, Rowan had suddenly become dangerous.

"That suppressor stone of yours won't stop me, Captain Fisher. It'll protect you and Hawk from my magic, but it's not powerful enough to prevent me leaving any time I choose. I should have killed you both when you first came here. But I made the mistake of going by appearances instead of reputation. I really didn't think you had the brains to work out what was going on. By the time I realised you'd earned your reputation, it was too late to attack you directly. That would have been too obvious. Even Tomb might have noticed something. I tried using the Dark Men against you, but I couldn't match your training as fighters."

"Rowan, what are you saying?" Tomb's face was pale and slack with shock. He made vague, fluttering movements with his hands, and there was desperation in his voice. "You mustn't listen to her, Captain Hawk. She's not well, she doesn't know what she's saying. . . . "

"Yes I do," said Rowan, almost cheerfully. "I'm guilty, Tomb. Guilty as charged, guilty as hell. I killed Bode, and the four Beings, and I'll kill a damn sight more before I'm done. There are no Gods on the Street of Gods, and I'll make them pay for pretending otherwise. I needed them. I needed them to be real, and they let me down. I'll see them all dead and rotting for that." She smiled at Hawk and Fisher, and it was not a pleasant smile. "You want to arrest this body? Fine. Take it. I have plenty more, and this one's almost through. I would have had to abandon it soon anyway; you just made the decision a little easier."

"I'm afraid not," said Hawk. "I thought you might try and leave your body for one of your Dark Men homunculi, so I had a word with Buchan earlier. He has the Exorcist Stone, Rowan. Until we decide otherwise, no magic will work in your vicinity. You're stuck in your own body. And you'll stay there until your trial."

"What are you talking about?" said Tomb. "Nothing's happened to the magic here. I'd know." He gestured quickly with his left hand, and a lamp on the wall lit itself. Hawk looked at the bright flame, and his heart sank.

He and Fisher looked at each other. "That shouldn't be possible," said Hawk "Isobel, go and find Buchan. Make sure he's got the Stone."

"That won't be necessary," said a slow, harsh voice from the doorway. Everyone except Rowan looked round in time to see the Dark Man throw Buchan's bloodied form into the drawing room. He hit the floor hard, and lay still. The Dark Man strode into the drawing room, the Exorcist Stone clutched firmly in one large bony hand. Two more Dark Men followed him into the room. They all wore the same shapeless furs, they were all heavily muscled, and they all had the same cold smile. Rowan's smile.

"I've learned a lot since I first started working with Bode," said Rowan calmly. "In the beginning, it was all I could do to handle one body at a time. But the more I practised, the easier it got. Now there's no limit to how many homunculi I can control at one time."

Tomb had knelt beside Buchan, and was checking his injuries with gentle hands. "Cracked ribs, broken right arm, cracked skull; probably concussion as well. How could you do this, Rowan? He was your friend."

"He would have used the Stone on me," said Rowan. "Luckily, for a famed duellist he was surprisingly easy to sneak up on from behind."

"We have to get him a doctor, Rowan. I can't heal serious injuries like these. He needs a specialist."

Rowan looked at Buchan unemotionally. "He would have used the Stone on me." She turned and looked at Hawk and Fisher again. "Keep your hands away from your weapons. I had a feeling you were getting too close to the truth. I had planned to have the Dark Men ambush you as you left here, but this has worked out just as well. Now I have all my enemies in one place."

"Where did you get all the Dark Men from?" said Fisher, playing for time and mentally measuring the distance between her and the mystic.

Rowan smiled. "I inherited them from Bode. He really was very talented. After I've had a chance to acquire his notes and study them, I'm sure I'll be able to create even more. I should even be able to produce copies of my original body, without the original's defects. There's a lot to be said for the Dark Men, but I always feel so much more comfortable in my own body."

"Buchan needs a doctor!" said Tomb. "He could die!"

"He never liked me," said Rowan. "He never even looked at me."

Tomb got slowly to his feet. "So. It is all true. Everything they said. And you're going to kill everyone who knows your secret."

"That's right, Tomb."

"What about me?"

"What about you?"

They looked at each other, and neither of them would drop their eyes. Hawk drew his axe, aimed, and threw it in one rapid movement while Rowan was distracted. The heavy blade flashed through the air and buried itself between the eyes of the Dark Man holding the Exorcist Stone. Rowan screamed in pain and rage as the homunculus crumpled to the floor. The Stone rolled away from his limp fingers. One of the other Dark Men started toward it, but Fisher moved quickly forward to block his way. She grinned nastily at him, sword at the ready before her. Rowan's mouth set itself in a thin, flat line, and the two Dark Men advanced, one on Hawk and one on Fisher.

Hawk threw himself at the fallen homunculus, put a foot on the head to steady it, and jerked his axe free. He spun round just in time to parry a sword blow from the approaching Dark Man. Sparks flew as steel rang on steel again and again. Hawk was forced back, step by step, from the sheer force of the attack. The Dark Man pressed forward untiringly, and Hawk's arm began to ache from the effort of parrying the blows. The axe was never intended as a defensive weapon. At any other time, he might have been able to turn aside the attack and launch one of his own, but he'd gone too long without rest or sleep and it was starting to catch up with him. His back slammed up against a wall, bringing him to a sudden halt. Finding extra strength from somewhere, he brought his axe across in a short vicious arc that had the Dark Man jumping backwards to avoid it, but he couldn't find the speed to follow it up. He moved away from the wall, and the Dark Man was on him again. Hawk caught a glimpse of the Exorcist Stone lying on the floor, but it was a long way away, and besides, he didn't even know how to activate it. He swung his axe double-handed, and tried to make himself some room to move in.

Fisher attacked her Dark Man head on, and the two of them stamped and lunged, their swords clashing and flying apart almost too quickly for the eye to follow. Rowan obviously didn't know much about swordsmanship, but with the Dark Man's strength and reflexes she didn't have to. All she had to do was keep up her attack and wait for Fisher's strength to run out. They both knew it wouldn't take long. Fisher was already exhausted from the long day, and the Dark Man was fresh and tireless. Fisher held her ground, as much out of pride as anything, but she was beginning to have a bad feeling about this fight.

Tomb faced Rowan squarely. Her face was blank and empty, but her muscles occasionally jumped and twitched in sympathy with the Dark Men.

"Rowan, you've got to stop this. Get out of here while you can."

"Not now, Tomb. I'm busy."

"Hawk and Fisher are Guards, experienced fighters. They'll win, in the end. And as long as they've got the suppressor stone, your magic can't hurt them."

"There are ways round the suppressor stones. I have more magic than you think."

"I won't let you hurt them, Rowan."

Life came suddenly to Rowan's eyes, and she fixed him with an unwavering stare. "Don't interfere, Tomb. It wouldn't be healthy."

"Your magic's no match for mine, and you know it. There's still time to stop this nonsense, Rowan. We could leave here now, together, and use the Dark Men and our magic to cover our trail. We could leave Haven, start again somewhere else. No one would ever have to know about all this."

"Yes," said Rowan slowly. "I could do that." She stepped toward him, took hold of his chin, and pulled his face close to hers. "You'd give up everything, to be with me?"

"Of course," said Tomb. "I love you, Rowan."

"I know."

She thrust her dagger into Tomb's gut, twisted it once, and then jerked it sharply upwards. Tomb's hands clutched at her shoulders, closed tight, and then released her as he fell clumsily to the floor. His eyes were still open, staring reproachfully at the ceiling. Rowan turned her back on him and slipped the dagger back into its concealed sheath on her arm.

Meanwhile, Hawk had got his second wind. He'd got more than a little annoyed at being beaten by a slab of muscle with no skills, and the anger had given him new strength. He brought his axe across to hold the Dark Man's sword locked in position, and the two of them stood toe to toe, glaring into each other's faces. Without looking away, Hawk stamped down hard on the Dark Man's instep, and felt, as much as heard, bones break in the Dark Man's foot.

Pain flared across the homunculus's face, and his sword arm wavered. Hawk spat in his eye, and the Dark Man fell back instinctively. Hawk took advantage of the opening to knee his opponent solidly in the groin. The Dark Man froze, his sword dropping as Rowan's mind tried frantically to deal with so many pains at once, and Hawk swung his axe in a vicious lateral sweep. The heavy blade cut through the Dark Man's throat, almost severing the head from the body. He fell heavily to the floor, twitched uncertainly, and then lay still in a growing pool of his own blood.

Fisher suddenly broke away from her opponent and sprinted across the room toward Rowan. The mystic opened her mouth to begin a spell, but Fisher was already there, her sword point at Rowan's throat. The Dark Man froze where he was.

"Drop his sword, Rowan. Or I swear I'll kill you now and to hell with a fair trial."

Rowan glared at her. Fisher increased the pressure of her sword. A thin trickle of blood ran down the mystic's neck as the sword-point broke her skin. Hawk stepped in behind the hesitating Dark Man and buried his axe in the back of the creature's skull. The Dark Man crashed to the floor. Some of the strength seemed to go out of Rowan, and her shoulders slumped. Hawk pulled his axe free and wiped it on the Dark Man's clothes. He looked to see Fisher was all right, and nodded, satisfied.

"I trust there are no more surprises in store, Rowan? Isobel, keep an eye on her. I'll take a look at Tomb and Buchan."

He knelt beside the sorcerer, and winced at the awful wound. Rowan had all but gutted him. Blood had pooled around Tomb and soaked his robes, but incredibly he was still breathing, shallowly. His eyes moved slightly to meet Hawk's gaze.

"Lie still," said Hawk quickly. "We'll get you a doctor."

"No point," said Tomb, his voice little more than a whisper. "I'm a sorcerer. I know how bad the wound is. I take it you beat the Dark Men?"

"Sure," said Hawk. "We beat them."

"Is Rowan all right? You didn't hurt her?"

"She's fine."

"Good." Tomb closed his eyes. Hawk said the sorcerer's name a few times, but he didn't respond. The man's breathing was so shallow that Hawk was sure each breath would be the last, but somehow Tomb held on. Hawk moved over to Buchan. He was unconscious, but breathing strongly. His wounds looked nasty, but not immediately dangerous. Hawk got to his feet and moved over to join Fisher. She'd taken the sword point away from Rowan's throat but held the sword ready, just in case.

"Tomb's dying," said Hawk. "Buchan is badly injured. They were your colleagues, Rowan. Your friends. They cared about you. Doesn't that mean anything to you?"

Rowan smiled briefly, but there was no humour there, only a weary disdain. "I never wanted their friendship. All I ever wanted was to be left alone. Nobody ever really cares for anyone else; they just pretend to, to get what they want from you. They don't fool me. I look out for myself. And you needn't look at me like that. I'm no different from anyone else; it's just that I have the guts to be honest about it.

"You can't hold me, you know. There are more Dark Men, scattered all over Haven. Bode had been creating them for years, selling his potions to subsidize his experiments. He had a horror of dying, you see. He thought he could live forever, through his doubles. But I put a stop to that. I had a better use for them. I still do. You can't stop me. The magic in your suppressor stone is fading, even as we speak. Soon it'll be cold and silent, and I'll leave this defective body behind and live again as a Dark Man. I will have my revenge on the Street of Gods, and there's nothing you can do to prevent it."

"Maybe they can't," said a calm, deep voice. "But I can."

They all turned, startled, to look at the doorway. A Dark Man stood there smiling, dressed in a cheap grey robe and looking somehow . . . different. He wasn't i the least muscular, being instead slender almost to the point of malnutrition, and his face held none of the anger that was a permanent part of Rowan's expression whatever body she was wearing. Hawk looked quickly at Rowan, but she seemed just as surprised as he was. Hawk looked back at the Dark Man. If she wasn't controlling the body, then who . . . ?

"It can't be," said Fisher. "It can't be *him*."

"It is," said Hawk. "It has to be. That's Bode."

The sorcerer smiled at them all, and bowed politely. "At your service, Captain."

"You're dead," said Rowan harshly. "I killed you. I watched you die."

"I'm afraid not," said Bode, stepping coolly into the drawing room. "Though you did have a damn good try. Perhaps I should explain. It's a very interesting story, and there's no one else I can tell it to. Besides, I've been starved for company for the past few days. I've been watching you all ever since my death, but I couldn't afford to be recognised. So I stayed in the shadows and waited for the right moment.

"I'm afraid you made a simple but understandable mistake, Rowan, my dear. When you surprised me at my home with the Exorcist Stone, you didn't encounter the real me; just one of my duplicates. I hadn't lived in my own body for months. I kept that somewhere safe, and lived in a series of homunculi. My experiments had become rather dangerous, you see, and I didn't want to subject my real body to unnecessary risks. So, when you activated the Exorcist Stone in my house after our little disagreement, you destroyed all the spells I'd set up, including the one that kept my spirit in the duplicate body. The Stone threw me out of the homunculus and back into my own body. All you killed was an empty husk.

"You'd probably have worked it out for yourself, if you'd had time to study my papers, but luckily my Dark Man watchdog returned from the errand I'd sent him on, and you left in something of a hurry, rather than risk being discovered. The watchdog was a rather crude prototype, and unfortunately given to insane rages, but he had his uses. You've really caused me a great deal of difficulty, Rowan. Once the Guard discovered the nature of my researches, I had no choice but to stay dead while I tracked you down. Establishing a new identity and starting over is going to be very difficult. Not to mention expensive. And all because of your obsession with the Street of Gods. I should never have listened to you in the first place. But . . . I needed the money. That's always been my problem.

"Dear me, listen to me talk. Rambling on and on, and all of you too polite to interrupt. That's what comes of being officially dead; you don't dare talk to anyone for fear of being recognised. So, let me get straight to the point. I want my duplicates back under my control, and I want revenge for all the inconvenience I've been put to. So I'm afraid you're going to have to die, Rowan. It's the only way. And of course I can't leave any witnesses. . . . Well, I'm sure you all understand. Nothing personal, Captain Hawk, Captain Fisher."

"Blow it out your ear," said Hawk. "You haven't enough magic to get past our suppressor stone, and you don't have the muscles you gave your Dark Men. So you can take your threats and stuff them where the sun doesn't shine. You're under arrest for illegal research on homunculi."

There was a soft, scuffing sound behind Hawk, and he instinctively threw himself to one side. The dead Dark Man's sword only just missed him, and plunged on to sink deep into Rowan's side. The force of the blow threw her back against the wall, clutching desperately at the sword. Her face was full of pain and horror, as she stared at the risen dead man, but she couldn't find the breath to scream. The Dark Man pulled the sword free, lacerating her hands cruelly, and stabbed her neatly through the heart. She sank slowly down the wall, leaving a bloody trail behind her.

Hawk swung his axe and buried it in the Dark Man's back. The dead body turned slowly to face him, unaffected. Hawk jerked his axe free, and he and Fisher moved quickly to stand back to back. All three Dark Men moved steadily toward them, blood still seeping from their death wounds, their eyes bright and knowing.

"I'd got a lot further in my researches than Rowan ever did," said Bode easily. "And I learned a lot more on the Street of Gods than I ever passed on to her. I really shouldn't have let her know as much as I did, but she seemed so keen, so interested . . . and it was a long time since I'd been able to talk to anyone about the advances I'd made. . . . Of course, in the end she decided she wanted it all for herself. Which meant I had to be disposed of. I really should have known . . . but then, I never was a very good judge of character.

"Still, she's dead now. Really dead. One of the things I never taught her was how to keep someone from leaving their body. But I know how. No more Dark Men for you, Rowan, my dear."

Hawk listened to the man chatter with one ear, while he concentrated on the approaching Dark Men. They moved slowly but surely, and held their swords with a confident grip. They didn't breathe, and blood no longer ran from their wounds. There was no doubt they were all dead, animated only by the sorcerer's will. Hawk thought quickly, running the possibilities through his mind. He couldn't get to the nearest exit, so he'd have to stand and fight. A lich may be unkillable, but it can still be stopped. Disable them by cutting through the arms and legs, or severing the head, and they'd be helpless. Hawk smiled sourly. Sure. As easy as that. But since he had no other choice; when in doubt, be direct.

He jumped forward and swung his axe in a vicious arc at the nearest Dark Man. Its unblinking eyes never wavered, and its sword flashed up to meet the axe. Hawk changed his grip at the last moment and swept the axe under the sword to slam into the dead man's side. Bones broke and splintered as the heavy axe head punched through the rib cage, throwing the Dark Man off balance. Hawk jerked the axe free and struck savagely at the lich's neck. It sank to one knee under the impact of the blow, and shuddered as Hawk

jerked the axe free again. But another Dark Man was already
closing in, and although Hawk stepped quickly back, the
lich followed him relentlessly, launching a sustained attack
with his sword, which took all of Hawk's skill to parry.
Behind him, he could hear the clash of steel on steel as
Fisher took on the remaining Dark Man. On the floor, the
first Dark Man was already getting to his feet again.

Fisher muttered the suppressor stone's activating phrase
under her breath again and again, but nothing happened.
Either the stone was drained or it wasn't powerful enough
to overcome Bode's sorcery. She scowled, and launched a
furious attack on her Dark Man, trying to fight her way
past it to get at Bode, but the lich stood its ground and
parried all her blows with inhuman efficiency. Sweat ran
down her face, stinging her eyes, and she had to fight to
get her breath. It had been a long hard day, and her second
wind had come and gone. Even if she'd been fresh and at
her peak, the lich would have been hard to beat, and as it
was she had to struggle to make it anything like an equal
contest. She had no tricks left up her sleeve, or at least
none that would work on a dead man, and she was starting
to slow down. Slowly the Dark Man moved from defence
to offence, and Fisher began to give ground.

Hawk and Fisher stood back to back, swinging sword and
axe with leaden arms and hammering hearts. Their breath
rasped in their throats and sweat soaked their clothes. The
near misses got closer all the time as the Dark Men pressed
steadily forward. Blood flew on the air, and Hawk and Fisher spat curses as here and there a blow struck home. Hawk
gathered the last of his strength and prepared for one final
lunge to take him past the Dark Man and launch him at
Bode's throat. The odds weren't exactly good, but what
the hell. It wasn't that far. Maybe he'd get lucky.

And then a brilliant light flared up, filling the room with
its glare, and one by one the Dark Men slowed to a halt
and fell heavily to the floor. Hawk looked quickly round,
gasping for breath. Tomb had dragged himself across the
floor, leaving a wide trail of blood behind him, and now

sat propped against the wall with the Exorcist Stone in his hands. The Stone blazed like a miniature star, too bright to look at, banishing all magic from the room. Bode looked at Tomb incredulously. Tomb smiled, showing bloody teeth.

"This is for Rowan, you bastard. Hawk, kill him."

Bode looked back at Hawk, and quickly raised his hands in the air. "I surrender, Captain."

"Like hell," said Hawk, and cut the sorcerer down with one blow. Bode died with the same incredulous look on his face.

"What the hell," said Fisher, tiredly lowering her sword. "He'd only have escaped anyway."

They put away their weapons and moved over to kneel beside Tomb. The Exorcist Stone slipped from his fingers and rolled away. Its light flickered and went out. Tomb's face was deathly pale, the blood at his mouth stark red against the white skin. He looked across at Rowan, lying still and lifeless, and his mouth worked once.

"I loved her, you know. I really loved her."

He closed his eyes. Hawk felt for a pulse in Tomb's neck. It was there, but so faint he could barely feel it.

"Is he still alive?" asked Fisher quietly.

"Yeah. But don't ask me how. You'd better go for a doctor; I'll try and keep Tomb and Buchan comfortable till you get back." He looked across at Rowan, and his mouth hardened. "Do you suppose she ever cared for him at all?"

"I don't know," said Fisher, getting to her feet. "Maybe, if things had been different . . ."

"Yeah," said Hawk. "Maybe." He looked away. "He deserved better than her."

And then a living Presence exploded in the room, suffusing everything with the glow of its existence. The Presence beat on the air like a giant heartbeat, or the wings of a powerful bird. A deep and desperate sorrow permeated the room, grief beyond bearing, until Hawk felt as though he would break down and weep at any moment.

"What is it?" whispered Fisher, her eyes bright with unshed tears. "What's happening?"

"It's Le Bel Inconnu," said Hawk softly. "The God that Tomb worshipped. The dying God. It's come here to be with its friend, in their last moments. So neither of them would have to go into the dark alone."

And then, in a moment, the Presence was gone, as though it had never been. The room seemed to echo with its loss. Hawk looked down at Tomb, and didn't need to check the man's pulse to know that he was dead, too.

Aftermath

The Street of Gods was back to normal again, or at least as close as it ever got to normal. The sky was a bright and cheerful blue, and reminded Hawk of pleasant summer days. As long as he didn't look at it too closely. The unmoving clouds and lack of a sun tended to spoil the illusion. Priests and worshippers crowded the Street, bustling back and forth and playing out their familiar roles in the never-ending game of salvation and damnation. Seekers for truth rubbed shoulders with wide-eyed tourists, all of them heckled by street preachers and badgered by concession stall-holders. It was all very much business as usual, for mortals and Beings alike.

Guard Constables and Brothers of Steel stood together on street corners, keeping an eye on things and swapping lies about their exploits during the recent unrest. The priests pretended they weren't there, and concentrated on the more important task of sneering at their inferiors and ostentatiously ignoring the rest. There was almost an air of carnival on the Street of Gods; a celebration of life, of chaos narrowly avoided. When you got right down to it, no one had really wanted a God War. It was bad for business.

Hawk and Fisher strolled down the Street, taking their time and enjoying the sights, accompanied by Lord Louis Hightower. People who recognised the two Guards gave them respectful bows and plenty of room. Hawk smiled graciously. It seemed to him he'd never seen the Street so calm and serene. There was still the usual sprinkling of supernatural flotsam and jetsam: a headless man crawling down the Street on hands and knees, a flock of birds that flew in an endless circle overhead, a laughing woman covered with bubbling blood, and burning coals where her eyes should be; but even they seemed content to keep to themselves and not bother anyone.

"I don't think I've ever known the Street so peaceful," said Lord Hightower. "One can only hope it'll last."

"I doubt it," said Hawk. "People have short memories, and from what I hear, the Beings aren't much better. Except when it comes to feuds."

Hightower laughed. "You're probably right. Still, the Beings have settled down somewhat, now the God killer has been identified and dealt with, and the priests are behaving themselves for the moment. I suppose your work here is pretty much finished."

"Pretty much," said Fisher. "The Guard sorcerers are searching the rest of the city for more of Bode's homunculi, just in case, but that's the only loose end. We're just hanging on here until the Council appoints a new Deity Division. Buchan's the only survivor of the last God Squad, and it'll be some time before he's ready for duty again."

"Indeed," said Hightower. "I looked in on Charles earlier today. He was looking decidedly pale, but much improved. Amazing what they can do with healing spells these days. And the delightful young lady acting as his nurse seemed very competent."

"She'll take good care of him," said Hawk. "Annette's very fond of Buchan."

They walked a while in silence, each of them waiting for the other to continue. Hawk broke first. "All right, Lord Hightower. What the hell are you doing here? Not that we aren't pleased to see you, but I can't believe this is the kind of venue you'd normally choose for a pleasant constitutional."

Hightower chuckled easily. "I'm here because the Council has selected me to be part of the next God Squad. I applied some time back, when I realised how bored I was with my life. The family estate practically runs itself, I've no interest in politics or the romantic intrigues so beloved by High Society, and even the Hellfire Club was starting to seem a bit childish. But Buchan had seemed happy enough with his work in the God Squad, so I applied.

"The Council contacted me last night and gave me the good news. Personally, I think it just goes to show how desperate they are, but that's their problem. I can't wait to see who they're going to choose as sorcerer and mystic. Anyway, in the meantime I have been given the responsibility of keeping the peace on the Street of Gods. If I'm to do that, I'm going to need people to work with I can trust and the priests and Beings will respect. I need you, Captain Hawk, Captain Fisher. What do you say?"

"Sure," said Hawk, after a quick look at Fisher, "we'll help you out. But only until the new Squad's ready to take over. The Street of Gods is an interesting place to visit, but I'd hate to have to work here."

STEVEN BRUST

__JHEREG 0-441-38554-0/$3.95
There are many ways for a young man with quick wits and a quick
sword to advance in the world. Vlad Taltos chose the route of the
assassin and the constant companionship of a young jhereg.

__YENDI 0-441-94460-4/$3.50
Vlad Taltos and his jhereg companion learn how the love of a good
woman can turn a cold-blooded killer into a _real_ mean S.O.B...

__TECKLA 0-441-79977-9/$3.50
The Teckla were revolting. Vlad Taltos always knew they were lazy,
stupid, cowardly peasants...revolting. But now they were revolting
against the empire. No joke.

__TALTOS 0-441-18200/$3.50
Journey to the land of the dead. All expenses paid! Not Vlad Taltos'
idea of an ideal vacation, but this was work. After all, even an
assassin has to earn a living.

__COWBOY FENG'S SPACE BAR AND GRILLE
0-441-11816-X/$3.95
Cowboy Feng's is a great place to visit, but it tends to move around
a bit—from Earth to the Moon to Mars to another solar system—
and always just one step ahead of whatever mysterious conspiracy is
reducing whole worlds to radioactive ash.
